MALACQUA

MALACQUA

FOUR DAYS OF RAIN
IN THE CITY OF NAPLES
WAITING FOR THE OCCURRENCE
OF AN EXTRAORDINARY EVENT

Nicola Pugliese

Translated by Shaun Whiteside

SHEFFIELD – LONDON – NEW HAVEN

First published in English translation in 2017 by And Other Stories
Great Britain – United States of America
www.andotherstories.org

First published as *Malacqua* in 1977 by Giulio Einaudi; reprinted in 2013 by Casa Editrice Pironti

9 8 7 6 5 4 3 2 1

ISBN: 978-1-911508-06-9
eBook ISBN: 978-1-911508-07-6

Editor: Tara Tobler; Proofreader: Sarah Terry; Typesetter: Tetragon, London; Typefaces: Linotype Swift Neue and Verlag; Cover Design: Edward Bettison; Printed and bound by the CPI Group (UK) Ltd, Croydon, CRO 4YY.

A catalogue record for this book is available from the British Library.

This book has been translated thanks in part to a translation grant awarded by the Italian Ministry for Foreign Affairs. (Questo libro è stato tradotto grazie ad un contributo alla traduzione assegnato dal Ministero degli Affari Esteri Italiano.)

This book has also been selected to receive financial assistance towards the translation cost from English PEN's PEN Translates programme, supported by Arts Council England. English PEN exists to promote literature and our understanding of it, to uphold writers' freedoms around the world, to campaign against the persecution and imprisonment of writers for stating their views, and to promote the friendly co-operation of writers and the free exchange of ideas. www.englishpen.org

Supported using public funding by
ARTS COUNCIL
ENGLAND

MALACQUA

'Any other woman would have been disgusted at the idea of switching from swordfish fillet to head cheese, from a ferry-boat to a frail little yacht. Any other woman, not her: do you know her way of thinking? Running away is shameful, but it saves your life. That is her rule for life, great lady that she is.

STEFANO D'ARRIGO, *HORCYNUS ORCA*

The characters and events in this book are purely imaginary.
Even if reality is overabundant in narrative pretexts, in any case.

INTRODUCTION AND PROLOGUE

And through the windowpane steaming grey thoughts following the sea, with Santa Lucia huddled behind him, hands in his pockets, listening to the silence of his silence, the gusts of the coming wind, and those leaves twisting in the street, down into the asphalt. From the street loneliness falls gracefully away to the sea, with dilapidated wooden boats, fraying lights, and ships in the distance, Punta della Campanella, and Capri, the great mass of Capri outstretched and remembering, as alien to the city as an undeciphered tower, close, yes, so close, and far away, too, with faded tales of women and emperors, with glimmering cargoes from the East and Africa, and grain, shiploads of maize, iron, golden sand.

In the restaurant they're talking about the paper: first thing they have to do first thing of all quite definitely is change the lot, everything from top to bottom. Drop Politics with a capital P and go back down into real life, the local news, the facts, the tiniest facts, of the people. Because the people go on living interminably, day after day, and they want to know the story of the monster on

Via Caravaggio and the whole panorama of trades union agitation and whether or not the shops are going to be open: and the paper comes to rest cautiously among the spaghetti vongole, with that red tomato sauce, the wine from Lettere and Gragnano, the poached octopus, oh yes, please, fruit salad for me. Outside the window the water presses against the banks of the Borgo Marinari, patches of diesel floating in the iris of a disjointed rainbow, and the boats are tied up too, the sea is now a stinking motionless pond, with the surviving gulls crying and crying: white powerful swoops against the sky and then back down again, distraught, with the grief of the sea that they carry within them, with that morning fear that turns grey, heavy, and black, implacably black, while beyond the glass the difficulties of the paper fly away, rolled up in newsprint, the smell of ink, leaden fumes. On the walls of the Castel dell'Ovo, Carlo Andreoli makes out the signs of the sea, the soft tufa eroded by the ever-rising damp, spurts of froth appear, stars flicker, fireworks in the distance, white fires moving, renewing.

Sorry, do forgive me, I have to leave for a minute, I'm going to see the Castel dell'Ovo. Just two minutes, what hurry is there? None at all, really, in this life that is forever slipping away: and now, for only two minutes, we want to turn it into a tragedy? Interrupt the undecipherable ebb, create the break, the moment of uncertainty: you on the one hand with your spaghetti, your poached octopus, on the other that mad, motiveless spark: sorry, do forgive me. I'm going to see the Castel dell'Ovo.

So he rose from the table carefully folding his napkin, and was it a goodbye?, certainly a motion of the legs, and the legs, inside the chest between rib and rib the sudden inexplicable question. While up above the blue stripes grew, they multiplied, they swelled, all of them, and black, almost black, rain, maybe: beyond the glass the brackish air, the smell of diesel, and that strangeness, such sad, sweet isolation, the others inside surviving and resolving, yes, resolving.

The way out on the right is by those little stone steps, then on to the little bridge, towards those unknown houses and the Castel dell'Ovo, with the cold, tense air, the parked cars, restaurant signs, and cars, and grey windows in the grey morning. Behind the Castello the sea, in front of it the huddled houses, disdained and held at a distance, not to be mistaken for it, oh no, not to be mistaken; no voices in the street, no children's games, only from the windows and the closed doors a slow whisper, a dark, mysterious susurration like that of people plotting, scheming in the darkness. A sudden scream would knock everything into the sea, everything apart from the Castello, perhaps, and perhaps this too: a labyrinthine, disconnected scream, a hiss desperate to interrupt, to cut through. That long hiss that arises from within Carlo Andreoli along with his thoughts, and he thinks yes, but in the glimmer the grey is softened, the dust particles fly briefly, and from the windows and the closed doors there still issues the sound of voices, an alert, suspicious whisper: streaks of blue falling to press down on the asphalt, fists clenched in pockets, waiting to wave, to grip. Until the eyes purr in the silence, that silence, with the thought that has fled, the straight road, with only the Castello, alone and deserted: the sweetest enchantment, as fixed as if it were dead. You looked inside: might it be waiting, still, waiting for death?

Carlo Andreoli turned back into the restaurant to resume the interrupted discussion and the affable conversation, and the red wine from Lettere and Gragnano, and the sated postprandial jollity. His gaze is confused by the sound of the glasses, the newspaper too, of my beloved newspaper gently moving elsewhere: I will come and follow you for this one day, I will consolidate my affection loudly down the corridors, and shouts, smiles, shouts, for the printers. And so he gets up with all the others, and they all go outside, the editor at the front, and before going back up Via Partenope, there, before going back, his head turns, his heart turns towards the Castel dell'Ovo. But it can't be seen any more, it can't be seen from here.

And for all that afternoon and for all that evening Carlo Andreoli stayed at the newspaper to work, and how slowly the time passed, waiting for the sound of the teleprinter, with deeply hostile friendly voices, suddenly unknown, and alone again he was, looking at the stripes of the teleprinter and he didn't read and he didn't understand, and away everything went, really everything: trip by President Ford, growth at Fiat, concert at the Auditorium and lock-out at Innocenti, actors and actresses trades unionists and politicians slid to the ground, an imperceptible sound. With that deep silence of the desk and that light, the printing arm paused expectantly, and something like a buzz came from within, a run-down diesel engine running calmly, peacefully, and then rose into his temples to press and knock: the undeciphered waiting? It was being born to rancour, to sordid thought, it bound his face, his features: the idea wide open within the unlikely idea: what?, the keys of the typewriter?, the blue lamp?, the fluorescent lights in the corridors?, what, for God's sake?, what?

And after the afternoon and after the first hours of evening, night arrived for him, with inky streaks and sudden gusts, the wind blowing up Via Marittima on the corner of Piazza del Municipio, and beyond, and beyond, all the way inside the port and up the hill. That cold wind that carries up the fire of the braziers, which embroiders in the shade of the street. The moment came for him, which turned out to be nothing, nothing definite, but it was something: from the Castello, the message had come imperceptibly but clearly, yes, very clearly, it had come down through the throat and into the middle of the chest just in the middle it had stopped pausing to remember. And Carlo Andreoli buttoned up his Loden jacket, turning up the collar, and looked around, and breathed in the street, saw the tram ahead with its lights flickering, the receding hiss of iron on iron, and then looked to the sky, suspiciously, to check the presence of blackish streaks, faraway gusts, and that opaque glimmer that gave off no light, not even a little light, on an evening like this. Ah, yes, alone in the middle of the street, with that faraway, faraway thought, however close. And in the end he got into the car, turned the ignition key, switched on the lights, yes, switched on the lights. He felt uneasy.

THE FIRST DAY

At seven in the morning on the 23rd of October, which was the following day, the news came first to Annunziata Osvaldo, 27, of Boscotrecase, telephone operator on the emergency service at police headquarters. After she had heard it Annunziata Osvaldo looked instinctively upwards, at the window with the iron bars, and outside it was raining, definitely, it was raining: the rain had started falling in violent spates at about three in the morning, at various points in the city the lights had blown, completely useless, the emergency teams of the Enel had also realised that they couldn't fix a thing if it went on raining as it was raining right now, and as it had continued throughout the night until the first light of a greyish dawn, sometimes violet in tone, resolutely pallid and funereal. With all that water coming down and coming down, and when you were about to say: there, it's stopping now, you didn't have time to open your mouth before the water violently returned, a harsh and predetermined rancour, an irreversible obstinacy. And at seven in the morning on the 23rd of October, which was the following day, Annunziata Osvaldo as ever couldn't understand very much; at the other end of the line the person speaking was saying nothing, he was speaking excitedly, literally eating his words and thus he expressed only a breathless residue: it has collapsed, the road has collapsed, completely submerged, there are people inside, the cars have been swallowed up. Before doing anything else Annunziata Osvaldo realised that the fire service had to be alerted, with the collapsing roads there was nothing to be done at police headquarters, to each his own jurisdiction, and in the register she wrote '7am, 23 October, notification of a collapse in Via Aniello Falcone, fire service to be informed', and then called the fire service. From the station on Via del Sole her operator colleague told her he was already aware, that a squad had been sent out, and perhaps it wasn't a hoax this time, and other alarms had come in from San Martino, not to mention the surrounding province, then Sant'Antimo, Afragola, Frattaminore, all spreading out in all directions, and Christ the city's really made of cardboard, is it possible that only a few hours of rain could do this?, eh, possible, it's possible, what are you going to do?, the airport weathermen should put signs up: rain tomorrow. Neapolitans, move to Rome.

And at 7.30 on 23 October the fire brigade reached Via Aniello Falcone along Via Tasso, where works were under way to rebuild the sewerage system, and going along Via Tasso the firemen looked up towards those fading lights. The water was already crashing down on the asphalt, filling the uncovered channels, penetrating the earth and softening it, turning it into a shamefully inert mess, a slurry of mud around the new structures of reinforced concrete, and they would resist, definitely, they would resist. When they reached the tight bend of Via Aniello Falcone, the driver was taken unawares: the chasm was right in front of him, four or five metres away let's say, and he braked in a hurry, and what the fuck!, the others said, what a way to stop!, and what the fuck!, what a way to stop!, said the crew commander in the vehicle behind. The firemen all got out with their feet on the ground and the commander got out and they went and looked and it was immediately clear that this wasn't a small matter, far from it, because the chasm occupied the whole of the road, on the right all the way to the overhanging wall – with dozens and dozens of buildings below it – and on the left that dark chasm engulfed even the pavement, six or seven metres away let's say, from the foundation of an old building immediately post-war, perhaps, its facade painted grey and its windows all wrought iron and fuck!, said the commander, this is seriously dangerous, come on, let's get going, clear the lot.

And the firemen passed through the hallway and there right in the middle of the courtyard was the porter talking to a woman who had appeared on the first floor. They were both saying things, but when they saw the firemen they fell suddenly silent, and the porter now only listened: but how: clear it?, what?, all at once?, but then it's dangerous, seriously dangerous. And a woman appeared on the second floor with grey hair, about 55, and said that she wasn't going to clear anything at all, she wasn't leaving her house, even if there was an air raid. She hadn't fled during the Allied bombs in 1943, so come off it, not for a slightly more violent rainstorm or a big hole in the road she wouldn't, and still from the second floor, two windows to the right, a distinguished gentleman in pyjamas and dressing gown hastily wrapped around him shook his head disconsolately and said you see, madam, if the firemen tell you to leave the building there's a reason, probably a serious one, they wouldn't say such a thing lightly, isn't it true that they wouldn't say such a thing lightly? The firemen said no, they would never say such a thing lightly, they were saying it because it was dangerous, yes sir, they were doing only their duty and nothing else, they realised, yes, of course, they realised. But the lady said and where am I going to sleep tonight?, in a hotel?, and at whose expense?, the City of Naples? But you see madam I'm trying to explain the situation right now. But there was really little to explain, because in the meantime in the middle of the road the crew commander was collecting witness statements and there were a few people who had seen and who swore: in that chasm there are now two cars, definitely, they were parked right there, you see?, three metres away on the right, and they aren't there any more, and when the road collapsed I heard a dull sound, a strange sound, and a woman's voice, definitely, a terrible scream, sir, a heartrending thing. Staring at the rope on the truck, down in the chasm which was pouring down, a fireman had gone down, Giovanni Esposito, 24, from Roccarainola, who said play out the rope gently, play out the rope gently, and the others played out the rope. But then he disappeared, and his voice fell silent, and two firemen appeared on the edge of the chasm to see and could barely make him out: he asked for rope, more, but gently, gently, very slowly, and those two firemen passed his words on and the men on the truck played out still more rope, ten metres already, no joke in those conditions, not by any means, and then the crew commander said all right, pull him up now, I don't want to risk anything until we know. The other firemen in charge of the case pulled up Giovanni Esposito from Roccarainola, who set foot back on the cobbles, and the cobbles came apart at once, and he lost his balance and slipped, but the rope was there to hold him, the rope was there, and he merely slipped, his right hip only crashed hard on the ridge, he had a brief raw pain from it, but once he was definitely up it had all passed, all of it, and he felt no pain at all, and said to the commander: Commander, there must be people down there because I heard something like wailing, perhaps a woman, but I might be mistaken. Then the commander went to the radio in his flame-red vehicle and told them to send out another squad, with planks, tackle, winches and various tools they needed to go down further, about twenty metres, maybe more, then he said to the driver inform the Municipal Technical Office and tell them to send someone and explain carefully how things are, then right away call the assessor of Public Works, alert the Prefecture, and while he was saying those things in the pouring rain a cluster of people with black umbrellas had formed, and they were watching in silence, and at the windows of the building were men and women watching. But what the hell are these people waiting for?, the commander yelled, I told you to clear everything!, straight away!, and he looked up towards the upper floors, but a violent spate of rain made him lower his head again and fuck!, he said, and from below the hood of his raincoat he managed to light a cigarette, and call an ambulance, he yelled at the driver, or two, and he added under his breath because we have no idea how things will go here. And as he said that talking to himself, what the hell, today of all days, my wife's birthday, he thought of Via Tasso, oh Christ!, Via Tasso.

At 7.45 on 23 October the uncovered sewers on Via Tasso had completely filled with that shitty rain!, when will it stop?, and now the water was sliding along the asphalt, on the planks of the roadworks, on to the pavement, and quickly escaping downhill, carrying soil and waste and newsprint. At the intersection with Corso Vittorio Emanuele it was really a raging torrent that was coming now, while from above, level with the Italnapoli cinema, Via Tasso gritted its teeth, and also gritting his teeth and muttering fuck off was Biagio Di Sepe, 45, from Avellino, who was determined not to give a toss and had put on his rubber boots, on that morning of 23 October. And he couldn't even feel that water that was now passing between his feet, but he certainly saw it, he saw it very clearly, and above all he saw a few metres higher, where the uncovered sewer had filled up: the water swelled and gurgled, it almost breathed. Biagio Di Sepe suddenly said: Under these conditions I'm not bringing anything into the shop from outside, let alone the oranges with the rain, no, no, I'm leaving everything right where it is, it will have to stop sooner or later, and right above him in the sky there was a long blackish streak, and it had been like that at the market too, at four in the morning, but he had thought it would stop sooner or later, it would certainly stop. Except that it wasn't stopping, it showed no sign of stopping, and what a shitty day, he said, and he stood there with his arms folded in the shop doorway, and then he lit a cigarette and stood and watched. But when he checked that dull sound he saw nothing whatsoever, he heard only that crash, and those stones on the ground in the middle of the road. Then he looked carefully upwards and there it was, there it was, he saw it, the eaves were coming away, leaning towards the street, as if in slow motion, then the building began collapsing from below, thundering down to the cobbles, with those stones jumping, jumping, with the dust rising before being caught by the rain and thrust down once more against the asphalt. And fuck, he said, this is going badly. And he no longer felt so confident now, the fruit and vegetables would be fucked, who cares, something major is happening here. And the van moved strangely, just a hint, perhaps he was mistaken, in any case it's a good idea to check, it's a good idea to check, losing the van is the last thing we need right now, with this shitty day presenting itself. Biagio di Sepe with his rubber boots went to his parked van, climbed into the driver's seat and checked the gear, and it was in first, but for some reason he put it in reverse, and checked the handbrake which was full on, but that handbrake had never worked very well, for how many years had he been saying: I'll get it seen to, I'll get it seen to, and now with all that rain there was no time to get anything seen to, he had to do something, now. And he surprised himself by turning on the engine. And the engine for the sake of turning on turned on, but he said fuck what did I turn it on for?, what am I doing?, not the foggiest, and then he turned everything off, everything again, I've just got to put blocks behind the wheels, that's it, blocks, and he took two big stones from the street and put them very tightly against the back wheels reinforcing them with a few kicks, and now, now it was sorted, right?, certainly, it was sorted, and he was about to deliver another kick, with that river coming down you can't be sure of anything, and I'm certainly not putting the oranges outside this morning, and he was about to return to his shelter. At that moment house number 234 twisted and leaned. And fuck he said, is the whole thing about to come down?

*

Carlo Andreoli drank his coffee in bed, resting on his left elbow, surrounded by such darkness that he couldn't see a thing, and lit a cigarette. The phone rang and at the other end of the line they told him all that had happened: the chasm on Via Aniello Falcone, two dead, two cars swallowed up, the collapse of Via Tasso, at house number 234, with the five people dead, killed in their sleep, the rain that was still falling, and if it went on falling like that there wasn't much to be cheerful about, and that was more than enough to wake him up completely. He went to the bathroom and put his face by the mirror, which returned it to him. And first he thought about the paper, of course, everything that needed to be done, the reporters that needed to be dispatched, the photographs and everything. Then seven minutes later he was back in his car, and the alarm had gone off, now, and the red light had come on. His head spun through the city, up and down Via Aniello Falcone, up and down Via Tasso. And there was the chasm, and there was the collapse, and all the usual things, and the people, and the mechanical gestures, rituals, and the press releases, the calls to the editorial office, and getting it all down will be messy and they need to move fast, get a move on, you can't go out without the news, you certainly can't miss all the trains, today, not with everything that's happened, imagine the mess. His head spun around the city seeing chasms and collapses he had known before, the weeping of mothers and relatives, the hysterical grief, the muffled, impotent rage. His head fled spinning, of course, it fled but then came back on tiptoe along narrow paths and built for him a cruel and inevitable presence: where is the ultimate meaning? In the stones of the Castel dell'Ovo? Where?

He left his car on Via Partenope, and walked on in the falling rain: beyond the pavement the stone bridge, and the castle, with the yellowish stones against an inclement sky, and that rain falling on his knees and his shoes all the way between his toes, the damp reached his brain, the water rose along furrows and circumvolutions, shapeless gelatinous masses breathed with the water, and the water from within reached all the way inside his iris and appeared in his nostrils, it fell from his nostrils and down from his lips it fell slipping in grey rivulets. Within the view of that watery grey now falling in spates, oh yes, in cold spates, the eye runs identifying the gaps between stone and stone. Come on then, wake up.

THE SECOND DAY

And on the second day it became clear. The rain had persisted; yes, it had persisted for a whole exhausting night, and reinforcement units had come flooding into the city: from the outlying districts in particular, Torre del Greco, Castellammare, Salerno, Caserta: and nothing else could be seen in the streets but the movement, cautious, not reckless now, of the fire engines, the red vehicles, sirens blaring, darting here and darting there, and people shut away inside standing at their windows, as if waiting their turn, and now they're coming here, now they're coming here. Waiting was a gruelling, progressive illness that grabbed you by the throat and squeezed and squeezed. You found yourself thinking that you mightn't die, but you wouldn't go on living, at least not like before. That slow, interminable rain had altered the outlook on things: your life would never be the same again, never again, because now any emergent life was conditioned by the water that was falling, falling, the water stopping the cars in the streets, spewing back up from the sewers and down the hill towards the sea, and the water was rising from the sea as well, its pressure mounting, and the waves swelled to smash against the moorings, and you would also have to say that on the second day it became clear, or rather people began to understand: perhaps this wasn't the rain of other years, other months, perhaps this rain here was coming from a long way away. This time the city's patron saint, St Gennaro, would manage on his own, poor old stupid St Gennaro, with that glass ampoule of his blood melting vexingly, dividing minds and creating confusion. All the people were pressed up against their windows looking up from below and seeing and noticing and following, and there was a long, interminable procession of water to cross. It choked up from the gutters of the fortress of the Maschio Angioino, whose marble frontage was reflected in the grey shadow of the water that flowed from the gutters, but it was no longer a defence, oh, it wasn't a defence any more, now it was in an anxious and imperceptible state of siege. And inside the fortress and within the high walls there was no one, and no one had any plans to go there, but faint voices issued from the deserted benches of the Baronial Hall, carried by microphones, so indistinct and defective that the words were impossible to make out. But they were words, words they certainly were, and human voices, ambiguously human, which burst outside in weird distortions, indecipherable sounds of sobbing, noises muffled and growing louder beneath the drops carried by the water.

The first few times an inspection was necessary, of course. Because the voices could be heard very clearly, outside, in the gardens and the streets around Piazza del Municipio, and that faint, broken echo sometimes reached all the way to the windows of Palazzo San Giacomo, breathless anxiety snaked like fear along the corridors, an obscure reproach, and the first few times a security patrol was required.

The Councillor for Public Thoroughfares sent out a select unit on an exploratory mission, seven policemen, seven, and the worried policemen went into the Maschio Angioino and saw the flooded courtyard spilling over with water, and the stone steps, the columns, and they went upstairs and into the rooms, into the corridors, they searched the Baronial Hall from top to bottom. Some of them remembered that only a month before they had served in that hall on the occasion of the council meeting, and they also remembered that it hadn't been much of a meeting, with unruly crowds of the unemployed beyond the barriers. And they searched and searched, behind the benches and under the stair carpets, in the phone boxes and behind the adjacent snugs of the bar, and the counter of the bar was in place, yes, beyond a doubt, everything was in place, and in fact they almost felt they could see the mayor, there, on the bench at the top, the fat mayor bent over his papers so as not to hear, because it wasn't his job, not to decide, because it wasn't his job, other people would decide for him, and not to offer rebuttals, because rebuttals highlight problems and make matters worse, and in fact they had a distinct impression of having heard different voices, each different from the last, yes. But search as they might, they could find no trace of any human presences. One would have to add that as soon as they stepped inside the Maschio Angioino, the voices stopped, and the sobs, and the distorted screech of words, and there was silence, now, only silence that was entangled with silence and with the ever-changing roar of the falling water. And after the most detailed inspection possible the policemen decided to go outside. They actually left, and went to Palazzo San Giacomo to deliver their report, and they were in fact about to explain that there was no one there, no one at all, and that was exactly what they were about to say when from the crenellated bastions of the Maschio Angioino something like a roar rang out, and a long sigh, and sobbing, and faint words, and voice and voices trying to say, trying to come out, and couldn't, they couldn't, and they echoed only as far as the street, and the grey strips of sky that looked as if they were plummeting at an angle, but they weren't plummeting, no, an impression and nothing else.

In the council room of Palazzo San Giacomo the council decided that another inspection was required. Above all because the voices could be heard very distinctly, so there had to be someone in there, inside the Maschio Angioino, and secondly because the population was doing nothing but talking and murmuring about this unusual event, and the press was asking endless specious questions, so it would be a good idea to give the place a better check, give it a better check, that was it, and this time it would be a good idea if the Councillor for Public Thoroughfares went too, not because of his specific skills, and what might those have been?, but to give an example, and to show the timid, the thoughtless and the professional intriguers that first of all there was really nothing to be afraid of, and secondly that the opposition should not delude itself about attacking the council on the issue of voices because there was no issue of voices full stop. The voices could be heard distinctly, that much was true, but it wouldn't have changed anything. So, on that second expedition it was decided accordingly that the Councillor for Public Thoroughfares would take part in person, along with Deputy Commissioner Armando Giovannotti of the Tourism and Traffic Department, and a representative of the Carabinieri. And the expedition was in fact about to leave the courtyard of Palazzo San Giacomo when all of a sudden a phone call came in from Police Headquarters. His Excellency the Police Commissioner had found out about the expedition and was in a furious rage, and expressly demanded that a functionary from Police Headquarters should also be involved. What answer would he give to Rome, otherwise, if they asked him to explain the voices? It was precisely in deference to this legitimate demand that the patrol of official investigators was joined by Dr Giovanni Castellano, one of the most diligent and well-prepared men in the government building. And meanwhile the rain came down, and came down, and when you looked up there was nothing to be seen but an irritating presence, consciousness consolidating that perhaps from these rainy days onwards the outlook on things would change: yes, perhaps the rain wouldn't only erode the asphalt of Ferrovia, the fragile terrain of Vomero, the soft volcanic stone of Posillipo. This waiting grew and broadened, it spread, and the issue of voices had moved from the small stories at the bottom of the inside pages to the front page, and on that day of all days, the second day of rain, the editors of the two Naples newspapers had each written scathing editorials, one entitled 'The Voices from Within' and the other 'The Voices from Without'. And in the simple matter of the voices they plainly discovered an opportunity to address larger and more delicate problems that went straight to the top. It was, in fact, in consideration of issues of this kind that the Councillor for Public Thoroughfares, at midday precisely, gave the starting signal. All the senior authorities got into their cars, the drivers roared their engines, the cars set off, amid the silence of the onlookers and beneath the pouring rain. Three hundred metres further on, beneath the portal of the Maschio Angioino, the senior authorities alighted, thus beginning what would go down in the annals of the city as the Second Exploration of the Maschio Angioino.

And on the city this veil of rain, and they were aware of the waiting, waiting as draining as an animal's agony, alive and dense as an interminable outpouring of blood. The horse lies supine on the asphalt of Via Partenope, the powerful cage of its chest rising as it breathes, and the silence all around is palpable, and from the horse's nostrils the blood gushes and gushes. There is little left to say: that it was part of a team of eight, and that on the sea of Via Partenope, along with its seven travelling companions, with the coachman, and with the gravediggers, it had set off on its last dignified job: the collection, carriage and disposal of the corpse of a man who had expired the previous night, in his bed, in his own sheets, with the breath of his children on his face. The horse, however, was dying alone, yes, truly alone, a horse on the asphalt breathing its last, his heart giving up?, what?, through the veil of rain that was coming down and fraying the city's edges you could sense the unease and the sad presentiment: life would have to change. And perhaps it was changing at that very moment. In the greyish weft of silence, the rain came down as a warning and an admonition, it came down and it grew, black regret unwaveringly consolidating between rib and rib, and in the bones that rainy dampness, and that disconnected noise that suddenly detached objects and people, built walls, and green partitions, and drove newly pregnant women into their houses and constrained them there, besieged.

And so it was that the Second Exploration was about to end in a second failure, nothing at all within the walls of that castle, nothing but the noise of the rain from outside, and search and search as they might nothing had turned up, and as the reconnaissance team had presumptuously stepped inside the voices had stopped too, they had faded, they had gone away perhaps for good, and everyone was demoralised and tired. At that very moment Vincenzo Mirasciotto, city police officer, was searching with his electric torch beneath the opposition benches. In the orange circle of the torchlight something lit up for a moment, and suddenly the voice resumed. Loud and tremulous, like a curse from a consumptive, it rang out around the vaulted ceiling of the hall, reached the crenellated walls and spilled outwards in the direction of the city. At the sound of that incoherent and unnatural cry, Vincenzo Mirasciotto found himself hurled to the ground, with knees trembling and hands about which he knew nothing: that he still had them, how to use them, whether to use them at all. The torch rolled to the tip of his right shoe, its beam now directed at his own personal belly, with its inlaid buttons and the municipal crest, at the blue of his uniform which he always wore a little tight because he thought it looked more elegant that way. In short, for a few minutes Vincenzo Mirasciotto was so bewildered that he investigated himself, his own destiny, the mysteries of creation, the unusual event. Slowly, though, a few minutes passed, and then he had to perform a check. And yes, Vincenzo Mirasciotto knew suddenly, immediately after his involuntary pause, that his precise task was to perform a check, officially, a check, so he was careful not to alert anyone, and why would he have alerted anyone right then?, and he regained his composure, he tried to rebuild his dignity as a city policeman, his manly determination. Once he was on his knees, with the torch gripped in his right hand, he leaned forward, rested his left arm on the floor, and what an unfortunate posture, he thought, on all fours like an animal, and he tightened the grip of his fingers on the torch, and mentally reconstructed the position, at the end of the hall, in the dark little corner, from which he had seen something and, also mentally, prepared to receive full in the chest the terrifying cry that had emerged from there, and I'm turning it on now, I'm turning it on now, he repeated to himself, but at last he made his mind up and turned on the light. The noise came, a powerful blast of noise as if from a crowd, an indistinct roar of voices, a crash of thunder in the night. It came, that dark sonorous presence like a Great Almighty Voice and his body, the body of a simple city policeman, was hurled backwards. It was certainly something strange and terrifying, it did him no harm, oh no, it just crashed out that powerful, plaintive thunder. Like a loud groan, an anguished cry, what?, dear God!, what? Vincenzo Mirasciotto, amidst all that racket, and then that disconcerting, cold silence, was left on the ground with his hand on his chest, rubbing it level with his heart, oh, yes, his heart, and waited patiently to come back to his senses: he saw himself, of course he did, he saw himself lying there on the ground, his hand automatically stroking his chest, his body still disjointed as if the soldering had come apart. He saw himself, and was even aware of the cry that was moving away now, moving outside towards the city, and for a few minutes he was lucid enough, and as soon as he had heard there we are I'm getting a grip, now I'm getting a grip, he had really got a grip, and on the floor he went on reflecting. He cast his eyes around and saw the benches of the council chamber and the vaulted ceilings and the seats and the Mayor's chair and his other hand clutching the torch, and he stayed firmly on the floor with a half-smile, and intensely bright lights went out one after the other, and then he felt alone, utterly alone. But much as that unusual condition weighed upon him – would his outlook on life change over the days to come? – he clearly felt the corners of his mouth stretching in a smile of self-satisfaction: oh a half-smile, just a half-smile, fine, but: he knew. Certainly, he knew now, and he had seen, and without a doubt he had seen very clearly, even if he didn't understand, even if he couldn't understand, but where seeing was concerned he had seen. For another few minutes he stayed down there, sitting, with the benches in front of him and that thing in the far dark corner, and the torch clutched tightly in his fingers. And it was only after thinking, after thinking and thinking again, that he made his mind up at last: he got to his feet, smoothed the creases in his jacket, examined the tips of his shoes, and finally, unsteadily, crossed the Baronial Hall on the corridor side. In his mind he repeated everything to himself, as he would tell it: and in fact, when the time came the explanation came out quite clearly. Mr Councillor, strange and unbelievable though it might seem to you, I think I have identified the source of the voices, except that it isn't easy to say, it isn't easy to say, and perhaps it would be better if we all went down there once more. And now there was a tremor in those words of his, and down the windows came the noise of the falling rain, and each one of them reflected: he would certainly remember that day, and who could ever forget such a day? And in the end Vincenzo Mirasciotto said it straight and clear: Mr Councillor, the source of the voices is a doll. And as he said it, he himself noticed the suspicion on the part of the others, and the disbelief, and the sarcasm. Was it possible that he might have been dreaming? No, he certainly hadn't been dreaming, no sir. There was that deep, enfolding silence, and from outside a noise of rain perfectly identical to the noise of rain from the previous day, and it had seemed for a moment as if nothing was going to change, really nothing, and difficult though the situation was, it was still under control, and the authorities in charge of security had plainly implemented their security, hadn't they? And until that moment nothing had escaped the mechanics of the predictable, nothing at all, but a doll, come on, now, a doll! Certainly, they were all thinking it, oh, how they were thinking it, but no one said it, no one, and in fact they all stayed silent, heads lowered, studying the tips of their shoes, and in the end there was nothing left but to say let's go. They left, in fact, in silence, only the sound of the heels of their shoes tapping out a rhythm in that ridiculous void with its high vaulted ceiling. With that sound still echoing they walked down the long corridor, and climbed the wooden stairs of the council benches, and then went down to the opposition benches, and the Councillor of Public Thoroughfares, who until that moment had been guiding the delegation towards the new evidence, now nodded to Vincenzo Mirasciotto, who was walking ahead of him, to indicate that he alone knew the place. Vincenzo Mirasciotto, a simple city policeman, said yes sir, and he advanced into the second row of benches, and once he had reached the third bench he stopped, sank to his knees and went down on all fours. Looking as he had done before, he tried to make something out in the darkness, and he could make out nothing but the same dark darkness as before. He nodded respectfully towards the councillor, moving slightly aside as if to say dear Mr Councillor, if you want to see, you too can go on all fours like me. The councillor did not object, and all the others, the members of the delegation, even though no one had asked them, all knelt on the floor and went down on all fours, scraping their knees and the palms of their hands, and discreetly colliding, and inadvertently jostling one another.

Is it dangerous? asked the councillor. Ah, no, I don't think so, and then he explained what had happened with the torch and the start of a scream. In the end it was clear to the councillor and a little less clear to the others: if they wanted to look in the dark corner, they need learn to bear the scream that would emerge. A loud scream, loud enough, but nothing dangerous, and in the end it was bearable, yes, definitely, just a bit bewildering, nothing more, otherwise it was really quite bearable. But even a scream foreseen is not a thing to be trifled with. The councillor wondered to himself whether he could ask police officer Vincenzo Mirasciotto to reach an arm into the corner and bring that thing out with his hands. But suddenly he realised: there was no need, no, there was no need. If someone had that possible duty to fulfil, that that someone was him in person, the Councillor for Public Thoroughfares, and he also realised that he didn't feel like it, he really didn't, and considering that in the gap in the bench there was room for another head as well, he called the Deputy Commissioner for Tourism and Traffic to come and join them. The three of them stood there apprehensively without saying a word, and in the end, when they could put it off no longer, the councillor informed Mirasciotto that they were ready, so he could turn on his torch as he had done before. Vincenzo Mirasciotto explained: there isn't time to see properly, just a second, a fraction of a second, and then the voices come, and you have to be ready, you have to be ready. For a moment the sound of rain was heard, streaming down the windows, and then the nod of agreement came: in the silence Vincenzo Mirasciotto lit the torch, pointing it right into the dark corner. And a groan came from it, deafening as if from a bloody wound reopened. A long, heart-rending cry as if from a multitude, which erupted outside the hall and made its way down to the courtyard, and climbed to the crenellated bastions, and took flight from the summit, outwards, towards the city, and now the city became clearly aware of it, oh yes, very clearly, and this time no mothers gave reassuring caresses, no girls started with fear, and in the end it was not as it had been when the cries had been heard before, no, this time everyone very clearly understood the message, which came clearly and distinctly like the long-ago waters of the Sebeto River: a multicoloured, heart-rending message that since that day – and it was the second day of rain – has remained hidden and locked away in the depths of their chests. Then the city was forced to lower its eyes, and those eyes looked at hands held firmly in laps, firm and sick as if afflicted with an illness and there was no illness, and the city gathered itself together in its thoughts of urban revitalisation, and carried out investigation, and it went on thinking firmly again, and the greyish streaks that crossed the sky of Posillipo were the same as the ones in Camaldoli and Ferrovia and San Giovanni a Teduccio and Materdei and La Sanità and Santa Lucia and Vomero, and from those streaks water fell with slow composure and water penetrated the gaps between stone and stone and water plunged slowly to dig, and it dug, and cut, and dug, and cut, and now the defences were disappearing, the cement was crumbling, supporting columns sent up desperate cries for someone to support them because they were about to give, yes, they were about to give: not suddenly, not immediately, and not from one day to the next, but they would give: and who will resist the water that falls and seeps and digs and cuts? Who created a hand so big that it can collect this water in its palm? And at that moment the city realised, and a cold, soft shiver ran through it, and the discs of the spinal column each knew for themselves and they were becoming disjointed and those bones were becoming disarticulated now, they were becoming disjointed, and shoulder blade and collarbone and the breastbone, the bearing structure was giving, and that will to live was giving too: what would happen?, what?, a universal flood to wipe everything out and start from the beginning?, an unknown rainbow irregular in its line and form?

Carmela Di Gennaro, who sold contraband cigarettes, sadly reflected that by now she had little left to sell, and that one day or another the water was bound to reach even those boxes of hers that she had hidden under her bed. The water would penetrate the soft plastic sheet and the coloured cardboard, and through the wrapping of each pack it would reach the filter and the tobacco and one day an inert spongy mass would certainly be all that remained of these cigarettes that now she couldn't sell because of the rain and because in the street there was no one, no one any more. The men had begun to desert the offices and factories, the banks and offices. It wasn't fear, it wasn't that, just a sad presentiment, a consid-eration that had withdrawn into her joints to recreate a different system. And what system could Carmela Di Gennaro have penetrated?, what different life would she live with her cigarettes?, with those packs and packages hidden under the bed, with that smell of rain entering her nostrils. She glanced at her burning stove to check that it was working well, and with her left hand she lifted the curtains slightly. In her iris she caught greyish images of rain coming down and coming down.

By now it was clear to all the authorities, clear as the now-forgotten sun, that there was no way of removing the doll from that dark corner. Perhaps it could have been taken, perhaps, but who felt like assuming that responsibility? What would happen if only a single hand extended to touch it, to test its consistency? And in short perhaps he was not stupid enough to risk the unforeseeable when by other means and different contrivances the question might have been equally resolved? So it was, and the Councillor for Public Thoroughfares at that precise instant also realised: it could be drawn out no longer, it wasn't possible now. However much authority he had, it was not sufficient, and in short there were others, higher up, and different in terms of rank and competence. The councillor, at that precise moment, decided to wash his hands of the matter, and to alert as they say the relevant bodies. That involved an initial obstacle not inconsiderable in extent: who is responsible, within the City of Naples, for a doll which, when lit by a torch, emits superhuman voices and long heart-rending groans as though of multitudes? To others perhaps this question would have seemed insurmountable, and beyond a practicable solution, but the pragmatic mind of the Councillor for Public Thoroughfares immediately grasped the solution, which was in any case within arm's reach: he would alert everyone, yes, really everyone, from the Mayor to the Commander of Police of Naples II, from the Prefect to the Commander of the Territorial Army, from the Communal Medical Officer to the Press Organisations, from the Chief of Police to the Commander of the Financial Police, from the Land Registry Office to the National Library, from the President of the Regional Council to the Provincial President, from the Councillors' Offices to the Museum of San Martino, from the Chamber of Commerce to the National Association of Medical Orderlies, from the President of the Regional Assembly to the Office of Antiquities of the Region of Campania, from the Office of Taxation to the Maritime Docks Board, from his Most Reverend Eminence the Cardinal to the President of the Association of Industrialists of the Province of Naples, and so on saying that he did not want for any reason in the world to find himself in trouble, in big trouble, over a doll like that. Which might not even have been a doll. But in the end the thought of what it really was had become secondary, the primary and fundamental necessity had now become a General Alert. The all-encompassing liaison work took several hours. In the meantime, very quickly, evening fell, with the rain that was coming down and coming down, with the rain and the darkness so dense that people couldn't see each other now and there probably wasn't anything to see anyway, and the unease was growing because so little could be seen, and Enel squads were on the road day and night – and this was the second day of rain – to reopen access where possible. The same Prefect had promptly interceded with the General Direction of the Fifth Zone so that the Office of System Recovery could engage as rapidly as possible. He had explained that the unease also went beyond the actual event itself, it was both psychological and political, that the masses must not be left in the dark, because darkness foments disorder and destroys respect for hierarchies. Once the General Alert had been issued in full, the authorities convened at the Maschio Angioino, and outside it they set up a police patrol, and don't let anyone through, you hear me?, I don't want anyone here, not even God Almighty!, in a loud and imperious voice in the silence, he heard that voice echoing within him, he felt it like a tremor in the depths of his throat. And in short when the police patrol had been properly set up, Vincenzo della Valletta, army brigadier, reckoned angrily that now they would stay outside and in that rain for who knows how long, if he knew the Superior Officers. The Superior Officers always put them somewhere, their inferiors, and then forgot about them, inevitably, and it wasn't so much because of the rain that he was annoyed by the whole affair, as indisputably because of that cruel forgetfulness to which he was forced to adjust every time he was called out on garrison duty, and fuck!, you can't spend your whole life waiting, and who do you think is going to come here to the Maschio Angioino, at this hour, with the rain coming down and coming down and the city deserted? Vincenzo della Valletta reckoned that in any case he was thinking nonsense: the Prefect had spoken clearly, had he not?, extremely clearly. Or perhaps he wished to question the orders of the Prefect? And besides: at his age?, after a whole life of blind devoted loyal obedience? Let us put it quite clearly, Vincenzo della Valletta: might it not be the case that the rain over these last few days has gone to your brain?, do you realise that at the age of 52 you don't even question your own wife?, you don't challenge anything or anyone, do you realise that? Vincenzo della Valletta, your age is over, it has gone, gone forever, you are left with your uniform, so look after it, and fuck right off and stay on duty with the rain coming down and all the rest of it. The rain was in fact coming down with violence, a coordinated precipitation slightly more dense than it had been in the morning. It had intensified, in short, and it seemed sometimes to respond to gusts of wind. Some had thought that the wind, yes, if the wind had risen up, perhaps strong and violent, perhaps then the rain would have stopped, perhaps it was a remote possibility, if the wind had risen. But it was soon clear that this was nothing but an impression, and an erroneous impression, what was more, because the rain was falling in torrents just as it had done the previous day, and there was nothing to observe or to record, nothing whatsoever, apart perhaps from the disarming bureaucratic regularity of the falling rain, beating down on the leather of their boots, and their boots were unmoving. Within the Maschio Angioino in the meantime a decision had been made which involved certain unknown factors and some calculated risks, truth be told, but in the end after lengthy confabulations it had appeared clear to one and all, clear and most pressing: that things could certainly not continue like this. The same bomb-disposal experts who had been dispatched to this spot could do nothing but light one cigarette after another and wait for the Appropriate Offices to make their decision. After a small meeting among the Higher Authorities, a decision had at last been taken and it was if nothing else a starting point, and this was what had been decided: that the bench beneath which the thing had been hidden would be broken up and removed forthwith, respecting the niceties and precautions of the case, and that, without moving or touching the mysterious doll, the wood of the benches would be taken outside, in such a way as to bring the thing to light without at the same time causing any traumas or shocks. It was clearly a provisional decision, perhaps even slightly too political a decision, but dear sirs let us take into account the supreme responsibilities that each one of us bears upon his shoulders, let us take into account the delicacy of the problem, let us ponder well the consequences that might be unleashed by an inappropriate action, and let us then do what at this point in time remains within our scope: to bring the doll to light. If nothing else, we will be able to take a closer look at it, and it may also be the case that by bringing the doll to light we will at last have a key to its interpretation. Because here no one believes in ghosts and dolls, so an explanation will be forthcoming, oh we will see such a thing, you can be sure of it. And when the agreement had been reached and established once and for all, two carpenters from the Municipality of Naples approached the bench with their tools. They studied its composition, its structure, the nature of the wood, the hinges, the nails, the type of glue which in places brought the planks together, and then they began to dismantle it. Always being careful to dismantle it gently, because not only was there a danger, obviously, if no one had previously attempted to approach and their intervention had become necessary, but above all they were working in the open, that is beneath the watchful eyes of the Supreme Authorities, and how were they going to complete the task at hand, for example, if even the slightest of their actions were to determine anything unusual or generally inauspicious? This mission was not to be taken lightly, far from it. With these thoughts silently mulled and ruminated upon, the two of them knelt down to work for about twenty minutes, with all the care and delicacy required, and in the end it was clear, not least and most of all to the Supreme Authorities that it had been a job well done, a job very well done, in fact, with prudence and exactitude. And the Prefect, who was following the work attentively, was on the point of saying something about the accuracy and exactitude of their intervention, and in fact he had already parted his lips, and his tongue had moved from his palate, and in short all that was missing was the vibration of the vocal cords, when the panel was removed, yes, once and for all. The panel was removed. And the doll was seen. And it was also seen without further ado that the doll was nothing but a doll. Black of hair and pale with a bluish hue, with a floral dress, the flowers white yellow and green, the little arms uncovered, and among the hair velvet ribbons. And that fixed doll's gaze, with the dark pupil, and black rather than dark, black, profoundly dark. And fixed were those eyes like doll's eyes with that impression of profundity. As if something were disappearing into the distance, fleeing, fleeing. There was curiosity around. And fear, too, disguised as sarcasm. Nothing was heard in the vast hall for the first thirty seconds, nothing at all, and that silence, so irreparably silent, assumed physical form and pressed down on their backs, everyone felt its weight upon their eyelids and their knees. An airborne jellyfish, a transparent dream.

Rumours circulated, subsequently, on that second day of rain, that men were rebuilding themselves as men and the Higher Urban Authorities would soon once again become the Higher Urban Authorities. It also became clear, subsequently, that nothing disastrous was forming on the horizon, nothing at all, because the Appropriate Offices were keeping watch as they always did. The vague dot on the horizon was not a Greek trireme or a pirate schooner, it was nothing but a battered cargo ship transporting ferrous materials. It would continue along the route it always travelled, and berth at the usual time at the usual dock. The sailors would turn off the engine as they had always done in the past, and would throw the cables, and then it would be unloaded, certainly it would be unloaded as ever, and the scrap would continue on its way on fume-spewing lorries, and the boat would resume its route, so everything would be normal and there was nothing to worry about. If that does not happen, if people are worried, well, never go beyond thirty seconds, please, don't go beyond that. And from the doll lying still on the wooden tables, the Prefect's eye flew temporarily to the tip of his shoes and temporarily his lips had an imperceptible wrinkle and then his eye came back sharp and sure to say that it had got late now. And that no one was to touch anything. Tomorrow we will come back and look at things calmly. And we will talk of it to no one, please, particularly the press. What would the population think? Let us always remember the population, my dear friends. And here for the moment let us leave everything as it is, and now you should leave and no one I mean no one will have permission to enter this room until tomorrow. We for the moment are going to the Prefecture for a small meeting. The police patrol will remain in its place. If they are to do guard duty let them do it, but no one I say no one is to come in here until tomorrow morning. It was extremely clear to everyone present at that moment that the Prefect had assumed full responsibility, and that he himself was not now the man to act, but the legitimate representative of the legitimate government and of the state, and even if some people had reservations about the government, well, so be it, my dear friends, but it is not appropriate to have reservations about the state, the state is us, we are the state, etcetera etcetera. In short, these thoughts were broadly similar enough for everyone, and everyone agreed, and everyone made for the exit and then they stopped, at that moment, to consider the rain which was coming down, and the displaced water that was invading the courtyard, the streams of water rushing along the walls below the crenellated bastions, from the corners, from the recesses of the windows. That rain was coming down with an intensity that was not the same as it had been that morning, or the day before. It had grown in force, yes, certainly, it had grown, perhaps imperceptibly, perhaps by a small amount, but it had grown. And it was very clearly apparent, all of it, just as it all was distinctly apparent, in the air, that the following day would be similar in every respect, meteorologically speaking, to this day, the second day of rain, and the first that had come before, which no one had forgotten, oh no, no one at all. And it was with these considerations in mind that the Higher Urban Authorities got into the cars that had been waiting with the drivers who had been waiting inside them. The cars set off with a gentle roar of their engines, and each one of them noticed with pleasure: from the moment when the bench had been dismantled and the doll brought to light, from that moment no fearsome voice had fallen again upon the city, none at all. Perhaps no voice like that one would come down, perhaps no such voice, ever again. There were things, however, that remained to be considered, oh, my, there were things that remained!, and on the other hand the small meeting in the Prefecture had been organised with that precise purpose in mind. When the Higher Urban Authorities were gathered together at the long table of the audience room in the Government Building, before any other business was attended to the Prefect called Luisa Sorrentino and told her to make herself comfortable somewhere and record all interventions in shorthand. Because he had the firm and resolute intention to preserve the most detailed possible minutes of that meeting. Those minutes would also have to serve as the basis for the official communication to the Ministry of the Interior, if there was going to be such a communication. Luisa Sorrentino, who had spent the whole afternoon looking out the window at the falling rain with a vague and indecipherable expression, Luisa Sorrentino concluded mournfully that it was going to be a long one tonight as well.

That evening so sweetly autumnal, with all that falling rain defining veils of omertà. Perhaps in all likelihood her boyfriend wouldn't wait. He would phone, perhaps, and he would understand. The tender enchantment of the previous days would not be repeated that evening, in fact could not be repeated in any way. Unless she decided to do what she had wanted to do for a long time: which was to leave. Yes, leave forever that boring house with her father and her mother and her brothers, that clean and tidy house, and everything in the right place, always, never entered by madness, never entered by adventure, where she saw herself withering away. No, it wasn't going to happen, and that was that!, what do you think?, that I want to spend my years looking in the mirror taking shorthand of the signs of my skin as it turns flabby?, the folds of my belly?, my breasts wobbling and then sagging day after day? Ah no, my dears, I'm not burning up the years left to me between a tidy Prefecture and a tidy house, and I don't want to have my thoughts in order any more, I don't want that in any respect whatsoever, I don't want to be wise, or have good taste, feel like a sad and balanced girl with her head on her shoulders, oh yes, her head on her shoulders and a gaping pain in her chest, and I don't want to carry as an abominable shame these two full and resonant thighs and the black, black hair that grows between my legs, and I don't want to hold them tight together and sad, those two still-girlish legs. I will burn up the anxieties and fears and dreads and my submission, my dears, I will burn that ever-tidy house. From the highest window of the Government Building I will wave dirty tampons and sanitary towels. Around town, stale and dried on my cheeks I will keep the sperm he spurts on me. I will find it stuck to my fingertips sticky and dried and wrinkled. Running my fingers over my cheeks I will remember him, and that thought will go with me through the hours of the day, and as I wait for the butcher to cut me half a kilo of beef, eyes lost in bleeding innards and shattered bones and the heads of goats and the snouts of pigs, I will certainly perceive once more that sweet tender sensation when it grows between his legs and then becomes hard red fire. I shall say it over and over to myself on public transport, in the halls of the National Museum, in the toilets at the secretarial office of Palazzo Salerno, in the chaos of Porta Capuana, in the silence of the church of San Ferdinando. I don't want to hear another word about ancient common sense, or about duties to be performed, or about models of behaviour, or about the example you have to set in life and the difficulties that you have to confront, and overcome, oh definitely overcome. I don't want to hear about this masquerade. My love, don't worry if I'm late again this time and you will stop calling because of your father and because of your mother and because of your brothers, my love don't worry, because when this evening's latest farce is over, and over with a good set of minutes, I will be the one who comes back to you, I will be the one who calls, and you will come down from your house without understanding, without comprehending, and you will have a stupid expression on your face, and hidden within you a slight tremor. You already know: women cause endless trouble. Probably you won't understand, no, you won't understand a thing, and you will read this anxiety and nothing more. And I won't reach out my hand to grab the stars that I once wanted to give you. I won't do it, my love. Because you're probably nobody too. And of course you aren't me. Who are you? But it doesn't matter, oh nothing matters: all that counts is that you will come close to me and slip my hand into your underpants, you will be completely dazed at that moment. And in fact that evening Luisa Sorrentino, who knows why, had made her mind up. Her conviction had grown on her. On that rainy day, the second since it had all begun, she had decided at last, really decided. This time she would do it. Oh how she would do it. And then, with that light, firm thought, with that deep seam of joy, with those laughing eyes of hers, she calmly made herself comfortable and sat down, and spread her legs, and then she rested her notebook on her right thigh and checked her pen by rubbing it on the white paper. And she was ready, completely ready.

So the meeting was about to begin, and the Prefect said to take note of the day, the time and the place where the meeting was taking place and the names of the participants. And in essence the meeting was ready to begin, when the Chief of Police said would you excuse me a moment, and everyone thought he was going to go to the toilet, but instead he left the hall and asked the whereabouts of a telephone and had a long whispered conversation and for a moment his eyes gleamed, and in the end he said fine, then, hurry up, get everything together and join me here at the Prefecture. Then he went back inside to hear what they were saying. But the things they were saying were obviously banal. In fact, they were evidently groping about in the most total darkness. That much was plain to everyone, including to those who were saying no, that in fact steps had been taken, results had been achieved. But they were saying nothing serious, nothing, and no one felt too much like speaking, because everyone was thinking about this rain that was coming down and coming down and sometimes beating on the windows, and because everyone was considering the matter of the doll, and laughing about it as much as they could, but then they stopped laughing and in fact it was like a worry from within, that lurked and gurgled slightly and certainly created a great confusion all over the place, and thoughts were slow in reassembling, in a truly remarkable fashion, and that unsettling presence of the doll was what everyone was really talking about, but no one was talking about it because no one knew what to say. The discussion continued for a miserable half-hour of painful invectives and without too much engagement, and no one got heated, and no one argued, and no one banged their fists on the table, and everyone was remarkably in agreement, not least because of the fact that until that moment nothing had been said, nothing had been decided. How sad, gentlemen, how sad. Only the Chief of Police sat still and silent, the wrinkles on his cheeks inexpressive, his forehead frowning slightly at intervals. At the end of that half hour a motion was announced by Police Headquarters, and the Chief of Police said excuse me for a minute, and he got up, and left the hall, and the others remained in silence. Because it seemed as if from one moment to the next some news was about to come in which he would, finally, interpret. And sure enough, three minutes later, the Chief of Police came back from inside carrying a large parcel wrapped in newspaper tied with thin but reasonably tenacious twine. He set the bundle down on the table, and while with his own hands he set about opening it, roughly tearing the newspaper, he said gentlemen, we may have something of interest here. Many of those present rose from their chairs, especially those seated at the end of the table, and congregated in the middle, and craned their necks to see, some scratching their heads, some adjusting their glasses. After sheet after sheet of newspaper, out of the parcel two dolls emerged. Bruised and disfigured and still damp with water and damaged as they were it was immediately clear to one and all that those two dolls were perfectly identical to the one in the Maschio Angioino that they had just left. Perfectly identical, truly. With black hair, velvet ribbons in their hair, their arms bare and their dresses covered with little flowers, white, green, yellow. Perfectly identical. That discovery was disconcerting in itself, but even more so was what the Chief of Police said, speaking slowly and in a low voice. Because the Chief of Police said that the first doll had been found on 23 October in the chasm on Via Aniello Falcone, along with the corpses of the two women who had lost their lives there and the two cars that the chasm had engulfed. And that the second doll had been found on the same day in another curious place, among the debris of the building that stood at number 234 Via Tasso, which had collapsed, as we all remember very well, because of the torrential rain on that day which was the first of the days of rain. The very day when, in that collapse, five people lost their lives, all swept away and killed in their sleep by the building as it fell to the ground. So what did those dolls represent, a sign of death?, what?

Carlo Andreoli took his things, his thoughts aquiver, his knees failing, and in silence the falling rain brought him back to earth. He thought about how life is not a dream, and other things besides. He turned up the collar of his Loden coat and beneath that vertical rain – 24 October, 11am – he thought about the tarmacked bridge and saw the two towers closed forever, and the faded metal sign, 'Office of Public Safety'. Beyond the pavement he made out his car, and the traffic on Via Partenope, the hotels that overlooked it, and that bright morning light that embroiders the rain and the flashing amber lights. And it was clear to him now, oh how clear it was: his precise duty was to get on with the work he did every day. Go to the paper, sort out the tasks that needed to be done, send out photographs, alert his staff to the fact that he planned to close early that evening because of the people who had died in the chasm and the people who had died on Via Tasso. And he became quite precisely aware of a dense and pathological attachment to this life of his which he spent surrounded by newsprint. That dense material, a fascinating and untidy amalgam. He reached Via Marittima, went upstairs, talked to this person and talked to that. The director wanted to know everything exactly, and in the greatest possible detail. The director was thinking of a fine and accomplished story, while he alone could see clearly: the story would grow a little at a time, and the details would come out one by one, and the victims' relatives, and all of that. The news would be reassembled to form an intelligible mosaic only later on, what the hell is there to say now while we're still on the case?, a chasm, a collapse, and seven deaths, and then responsibilities, of course, responsibilities. Legal communication concerning the falling rain?, for the Municipal Technical Office?, for the Mayor?, the Prefect?, the President of the Republic?, for whom? Then he said fine, I'll go to my desk, 24 October, at twelve o'clock in the morning.

At his desk he found the usual mess, the chaos, the confusion, and all those people shouting orders here and there. The few who were not issuing orders were trying to put them into effect as best they could, and in the end they got on with things as best they could, because you can't work things out anyway, and they haven't got a clue about anything but shouting in all directions and do this and do that, but in the end leave them to it. Carlo Andreoli still spent hours at his post. And he saw the recovery of the corpses of the two women in the chasm on Via Aniello Falcone. An elderly lady dressed in blue, with rings on her fingers and dyed hair. Her face was smeared with soil, her stockings clinging wretchedly to her legs, unrolled and laddered. The stocking on her right leg was unrolled all the way to her shoes. Except that her shoes weren't there. All there was wrapped around her old lady's arm was a fake crocodile-skin bag and inside the bag they found everything, yes, everything: identity card, gold chain with image of the Madonna of Pompeii, photograph of grandchildren: male and female, 340 lire in small change, banknotes totalling thirty thousand lire, hair clips, Social Services Medical Card, scrap of paper with various notes, tiny make-up bag, tram ticket from the previous day. And he also sees the recovery of the second woman. A girl, certainly, because of her jeans, her face disfigured by long open wounds in her skin and on her nose and on her lips and the soil mixed with the blood. That lumpy mass covered her eyes, came out of her mouth, and her fingers were injured and smeared as well, and her woollen jumper was torn too, and beneath it a white bra could be seen, and a pair of glasses without their lenses had been found beside her corpse. Carlo Andreoli shuttled several times back and forth between Via Aniello Falcone and Via Tasso, to check everything, to check everything, but he realised: how do we now ask questions of the civil servant on duty: excuse me, have you by any chance found a doll with black hair and a dress with green and white and yellow flowers?, how do you do it? On Via Tasso he spent some time following the excavation work in the debris of number 234, and there was a moment when a fireman gave the alarm: she's alive!, she's alive!, but sadly it was nothing but a false alarm, because she wasn't alive at all. And the fireman hadn't heard a groan, he had only perceived the idea of a groan. But that plaintive sound had not existed, it had not existed at all. Only cries and weeping, in the group of friends and relatives, who had been alerted and who were now on the spot while the family of the woman who lived in Rome was expected at any moment. They too would be arriving shortly, the people from the city of Rome, to check the damage, and fill their eyes with dust, and count the stones, and conceal their fear in their chests. Upon these things and upon these thoughts and upon these people there fell a rain which was the previous day's rain and which might also be the next day's rain, and the rain of other days to come. A discreet presence, as silent as possible, muffled the pain of the streams of water that fell and fell, and in the manholes of the gurgling sewers, and on that grey afternoon there was nothing but that frozenness of everything, and that falling silence, and those different inquiring looks, so different, that went searching and fleeing and coming back and beginning the search again, questioning the sky and the asphalt of the street, and patches of green in the distance.

The visit was composed and silent, even when the Higher Urban Authorities arrived. A formal inspection at most, without the expenditure of too much energy, but one reflecting the sorrowful interest of the case, a disconsolate and silent shake of the head. The friends and relations of the family that had been swept away in its sleep by the collapse of the house had various thoughts, and some thought with more faith and resolution that a share of the blame perhaps resided with the Higher Urban Authorities. For how long had Aniello Savastano been asking to be assigned more safe and decent accommodation?, for how many years had he been filling in forms from the Independent Institute of Public Housing to obtain such an assignment?, how many doors had he knocked at day after day? Perhaps that was the case, and perhaps it wasn't. Because Aniello Savastano, whose house had collapsed, had been told roundly and clearly by the fire brigade a month before, and more than a month. You must leave here, seriously, a terrible accident could happen. And yet in the end the fire brigade had left and had sent their report to the effect that the Municipality should take care of everything else, the removal, forced or otherwise, of the families certainly did not fall within their jurisdiction, oh no, their duty was only to carry out a survey of the case and ensure that the area was temporarily closed off. And the people from the Municipality were in place too, because Aniello Savastano had been alerted and warned several times to abandon the house with his whole family. This house could collapse at any moment, they had told him, and they had repeated it patiently several times. Aniello Savastano had asked: and where will we sleep if I leave this house? They had shrugged and said, my friend, we do our job and that's it, this is our remit, for matters concerning public housing you have to speak to the Institute, you know that very well, we at the Municipality have nothing to do with it. Aniello Savastano did know that, so he had gone back to the Institute, and a short fat woman with glasses and a sea of papers on her desk had said my dear Mr Savastano, you have not accumulated sufficient points, the first assignment has been made and there were people with larger families, and unemployed, and you're number 322 in the list. What do you want me to tell you?, try and have another seven children, that takes us up to ten, and maybe they'll decide in your favour. Aniello Savastano wanted to ask who they were but asked no further questions, and went back home, to number 234. Now number 234 no longer existed, nothing remained of it now but a few stones. Once the biggest stones had been removed with picks, the fire brigade started working with their hands, you never know in these cases, sometimes miracles happen. But the miracle didn't happen, not in the slightest. And when the work was completed, with the greatest possible diligence, and with that unbelievable water coming down and coming down, the silent confirmation came: Aniello Savastano, Maria Savastano, Ciro Savastano and Angela Savastano were dead, quite definitely dead. In the end two police guards stayed to keep watch over the ruins, because the magistrate had not yet arrived, and the survey and observation of the case were required, they were quite certainly required. Carlo Andreoli stayed there dubiously watching and within himself he heard an urgent question: excuse me, have you by any chance found a doll with black hair and a dress with green and white and yellow flowers? But how do you do that? How do you do it.

And on the night of 24 October, which was 25 October because midnight had passed thirty minutes before, he went up from the print room to the third floor, to his usual editorial office, and saw the corridors. The editorial office was deserted now, with only two or three people keeping an eye on the teleprinters, and the teleprinter rang at frequent intervals, more and more frequent, and the rhythm had changed now, and the turmoil had faded, the shouting. In the silence of that night, from the window his eye drifted towards the harbour opposite. The harbour was peaceful and silent, with very few lights still burning, and only from time to time a train's rattle in the silence, a rattling train and a few silent cars inside that silence. There was night, only night, floating over the telegraph poles, the neon signs. The trucks passed slowly along the street in the direction of the Autosole dealership and that slow regular movement would continue during the damp hours of the night with photographs of girls in the driver's compartments and fortune-bringing coral horns and towels folded in two and big pieces of bread and endives. That night floating around. And the rain that was now soft and light, a veil of white linen, and droplets transparently drawn, and now like a caress, the gentlest of caresses on the asphalt, and on the stones, and the wheels of the tram. Carlo Andreoli found himself following the pattern of the water and said perhaps it's stopping. Because he didn't want to think, he didn't want to. Above all he refused, he said emphatically no, it wasn't possible, and if it was, then he would understand, he would give it a meaning and everything would return into the Great Circle. Because you don't leave the Great Circle, no one ever leaves, and when someone does leave it means that for him there is nothing left to do, and if he leaves two stout young men with white shirts arrive and forcing him gently take him away and he makes himself comfortable and sits on the bench and smiles at the smiles around him and everything is white very white and from outside come muffled voices, very distant and very irretrievable. With a disconsolate wave of his hand he went and sat at his desk and stretched his legs underneath it before drawing them back, elbows on the desktop, and so many papers around and papers and letters and newspaper pages and headline blocks and lined mock-ups. He sat still and looked. And he didn't see. Except from within, that hum could be heard, and it was more apparent, much more, now that he was in the silence. And he dialled 257, told them to bring them a very hot mug of coffee. The boy came soon afterwards and for thirty-seven seconds Carlo Andreoli concentrated upon the hot coffee going down his throat. When he had finished he lit a Marlboro. His tongue followed the traces of coffee beneath his palate, his teeth were comfortably hot, his lips unfolded in the hint of a smile. With his cigarette between his fingers he sat and pondered. And he would have liked to, oh yes, he had been trying to for some time, but the key escaped him, escaped him completely, and nothing to be done, and everything was a confused and unrecognisable magma. There were only these facts, there, those facts to float upon and sink beneath and resurface again. He was striving after the impossible, he knew, he knew very well, of course he did, he realised entirely. He said to himself: no point in pressing the point right now: we have to wait, wait patiently, and hold back, and wait for the brain to work of its own accord. Something will come out in the end. Of course, something will come out. And appearing before his eyes now was the face of V, and gentle fingers caressing his chest, V, my love, your sublime body. This remained, this alone, the memory of a tender wound, and loins poised for inventiveness, her woman's breath in his ears warming his heart. This remained and only this. And no brooding, please, no brooding. Think instead of the cry that rises swells presses. And his phone rings, just at that delicate moment. And on the other hand there was the sweet and tender and caressing V, in Naples by chance, that very day, with her consort who had been supposed to join her from Sicily but who had not turned up. She wanted to say hello to him, certainly, say hello to him, and also meet, of course, meet. Because a woman cannot be alone at night in a hotel room in a city that isn't hers. How was he?, well?, still married? My love, he wanted to reply, my sweetest companion from Milan, we are a perfect match, tonight. We will light that fire for one more night, yes, we will light the fire for as long as possible, tomorrow is another day, and so much more and so much more he wanted to say. And instead he said: I'll see you at the hotel.

THE THIRD DAY

The third day of rain was 25 October, a day of pale and unhealthy spite, and consciousness accompanied the tremors. In the first hours of the day the streetlights flickered. Everything was extremely unstable and precarious then, in that moment, with that deep night now gone, of course, and the day that showed no sign of coming, no sign. In Piazza Sannazzaro five stray dogs wandered around, and the rain fell on to the water in the streets, and a faded hiss in the distance came from the occasional ship, and only the silence seemed comfortable. The silence that promised recovery, of course, and voices, people shouting, the rattling of trams, and cars, and policemen, and convulsive traffic. And yet nothing existed at that grey moment, and then the silence promised nothing, you have to go all the way in and plunge in if you really want to re-emerge, because it wasn't a pale silence, no, a sad silence merely, because behind the windows various eyes were alertly keeping watch, of course, keeping watch, and opaque with sleep they followed the still-falling rain, and that grey, Christ!, that discouraging, inescapable grey, and their breathing was strained and feeble. Nothing reached the asphalt and the volcanic buildings of Posillipo but sad thoughts, disjointed consciousness. Would it end? Would it ever end?

In his porter's lodge Salvatore Irace turns the newspaper around in his hands and images flee and news and thoughts go inevitably to the window and beyond, mingled with the streaks of that sweet, gentle insinuating rain, so stubbornly regular, regular, yes, and unremitting. Salvatore Irace reads attentively: a bridge has collapsed at Guardia Sanframondi. He remembered it, certainly, he remembered it well, along with all the houses and all the things and the people in his village. The harsh landscape, that wind that blew and blew remorselessly, so that on some days you couldn't put your face out of the door. He remembered it. The wind sliced his cheeks, stung his pupils, sandpaper dust fell violently on his eyelids, those red-blotched bony hands with their creaking finger joints withered. And Salvatore Irace wondered if it had really been worth leaving Guardia for this cramped watchman's hut. Of course his children were safe. Safe, of course, and thriving. Both at school studying, and studying reasonably well. Because he had told them, it's not all fun, my dear boys, your studies have cost me the sweat of my brow, and if you don't understand and if you don't study as you should I will tie you both to your beds at night and belt your faces, you know very well that I will, I will do it seriously, and your mother would do well not to intervene. Because I'm willing to understand everything, to forgive everything, in life, and I don't want to distress you, I don't want to do that, but get it into your heads that you aren't children of the rich, and that you have to study, and you have to improve yourself by your own efforts, you have to make your own way in life, and to build it you have to study, and study, and make sacrifices, and otherwise do as you like, but don't forget those studies. His two sons have to go to university. And get a degree. Of course, one mighty great degree. And you have to be doctors, because when you're a doctor everything is solved, absolutely everything. And maybe nothing is solved, nothing whatsoever, if you don't know what you're doing, but with a degree behind you, you have a lot of possibilities in life, yes, and bear in mind that your mother and I have another few years here and then we're coming back to Guardia. To tell you the truth we're a bit tired as well. Think about it, bustling about all day back and forth, ironing shirts all over the place. Do you think you can spend a whole life like that, do you?, what do you think?, does that seem fair? Salvatore Irace says to himself that perhaps that degree will solve nothing, nothing at all. He saw it very clearly every day, conversing with people who really knew what they were talking about. He shrugged. But what are you going to do?, tell my boys they've got to study?, tell them do what they feel because life's one big mess anyway?, ah, no can't do that. When you have children you have certain duties too. He remembered very clearly his father belting him in the face because he didn't want to work the land, he didn't want to, and instead every day he said one of these days I'm off, I'm leaving everything and going to the city, what do you expect me to do on this stupid land that gives nothing at all to anybody and you have to kill yourself with work? His father took him into the stable, tied him to the rusty iron ring and beat him with his belt for an interminable length of time. But there was nothing to be done about the belt-blows, they didn't persuade him at all. Oh no, Salvatore Irace was even more bullheaded than Antonio Irace. It was because of that bull head of his that when day came he didn't stop to think for as much as an instant and he said goodbye. And in truth he said not a word, because he left at night. Now with that rain coming down and coming down again Salvatore Irace turns the newspaper around in his hands and beyond the glass he sees his wife beckoning him because there's coffee. He gets up for the sake of it, but also sees that water, coming down and coming down interminably, and that desolate grey of the sky, and the daylight that hasn't come. He wonders at that point, he really wonders: how will it end? Because to tell the truth life has fled, now, and sometimes if he and his wife are left on their own there's always that dark presence, that sad thought of the life that was once in their life and has now fled; and when this happens he gets up, always, and says I'm going to the garden because I've got things to do. And his wife gets up too, and all of a sudden there is the sound of the open tap and the water flowing. She has started washing something. There's always something to wash, and dry, and tidy away. There's one more question, with this rain, and a sense of irritation. Nothing serious, oh nothing, but if something ever were to change. Here, all of a sudden everything might melt into air, everything destroyed, everything, years of sacrifice, of effort. But these are strange thoughts. Thoughts that bode ill. Salvatore Irace with his firm stride leaves the lodge, reaches his wife and they drink coffee. There is that habitual silence, in the hallway.

And 25 October was in fact the third day of rain. With this rain coming down like rain coming down. And everything normal, everything normal, in the streets of this normal city. So dark and confused, at any rate, and so unstable, so hard to interpret and even to perceive. There: let's say that not everyone perceives it, not everyone, and for some things will continue exactly as before. Except this little rain coming down. There has been the collapse, the chasm. But in essence nothing new, nothing extremely unusual, in essence. Because it is a well-known fact that when it rains there are collapses and there are chasms, and people call the fire brigade and the fire brigade comes running, and sometimes they fail to spot the corpse, and yes, all right, this time there are seven corpses, a mournful event, certainly, a tragic event, but also predictable, in some respects, from the ancient perspective of a city that lives its life in a continuous form of multiplication. If there is a multiplication in the numbers of children, and the unemployed, and women in the street, and people who need to be looked after, why not also the dead? Just this, nothing more. Of course, there are things that strike you, of course, they strike you. They leave a mark, they cause debates, and make people talk for several days. For a few months you remember everything, everything down to the smallest details. The fact is known even in the alleys of Montecalvario, even under the bridges of Sanità. Certainly from then on there will be someone who remembers of course, someone who remembers. One day it will be said: you remember the dead on Via Tasso and Via Aniello Falcone? Those poor innocent creatures? Yes, of course, they will say that, along with other things, and other facts. But let us also say one more thing, that life is in the end reabsorbed in tranquillity, collective facts are pondered long enough to be diluted a little and confused, and in the end, off you go!, in the end why do you want us to care about this whole mess and this rain falling as if it had never fallen before, my friends, let us regather, let us regather everything.

But this in fact would happen later, much later, for now there was a crowd of people on Via Aniello Falcone, precisely on the bend before the bend where the chasm had been identified, and there was another crowd on Via Tasso, just behind number 234 that had collapsed. These black clothes, and these umbrellas. With the water coming down and coming down. And rivulets coming down on the edges, and streaks of light grey, and the still silence and a murmur if you listened carefully. The story ran from mouth to mouth with a few distortions. And this event weighed down the men's shoulders, and pressed down upon the women's eyelids. The women wore wedding rings, that distinctive sign, that defence. Then everyone followed their own thoughts. If you leaned slightly against the low wall, and even if you didn't, in front of you was the city's expanse of stone leading towards the sea. The sea had fled in a grey streak into the distance, with faint lights, they too softened, level with Capri, Punta della Campanella, Sorrento. That thought collapsed slowly from below along with the filaments of the mourning garb it wore, and regathered, and blurred and that strange mixture was in the air, and in the drain covers, of death and of things to come, of painful consciousness and hope. How strong life is in the presence of death, like a conscious acquisition, and it rebels, and rises serenely to its feet to say no. And perhaps only with that black presence, which in any case drags itself inertly onwards, inertly or almost, and there might be much else to be said were it not right now for this dark and irritating presentiment of waiting. Because there is no point turning round and turning round again: but somewhere someone is certainly getting ready. And it is bound to happen. And perhaps it will be late, then, too late, but for the moment you were hoping for no one really knows where to turn. How do you say to your wife my dear wife everything is going to change now, everything, completely, so forget the new sofa cover, forget the phone bill, the hairdresser's on Saturday afternoon?

My dear wife, something's about to happen, something that I don't know and no one knows, something that will throw thoughts into confusion, that will relight the icy fires within the mind, and if that happens you won't be able to pocket the shopping money, tell lies to your friends and your husband, and neither will there be any point rolling on to one side at night and waiting for a hard presence to grow and press against you, my dear wife. But how can such things be told now? They certainly can't. Nothing can, for now. All that is left is that hateful embarrassment, and the thought of waiting. That presentiment digs and digs, it blows up the effluent from without. The effluent gurgles on the surface. Oh how it does. And that foul smell that it gives off. And everything was in it, yes, all pus within, and we didn't realise, or perhaps no, perhaps we realised very well, and perhaps we knew very well, but you know how it is, you avoid looking as much as possible, or smelling either. Because in the end we are all the same, aren't we?, all painfully the same. Then if there's this sewage of mine, there is also everyone else's sewage, right? One's sewage and another's are largely identical, there is absolutely no need to discriminate between the two. And it's the same with self-pity. Probably the best thing is to do nothing at all, with the great mess unleashed hour after hour by this rain that is coming down like rain coming down interminably.

With half-open eye fleeing the greyish strip of the sea and the little low wall a conscious thought returns: there is nothing else to look at: nothing at all: life lies in these umbrellas and in the murmur, in the water coming down and stirring the water. The sewers have been crammed and full for a good long time, and these rivulets which descend from Via Aniello Falcone and from Via Tasso to Corso Vittorio Emanuele are swelling hour by hour, and more water, in huge quantities, is coming down from Via Salvator Rosa and rushing downhill, Piazza Mazzini, and down to the Museum, and to Via Roma, and the water from Via Roma meets the water coming down from the Quartieri and from Corso Vittorio Emanuele, and the circle closes, a heavy and ineluctable circle, and that water meets in a circle and surges towards the sea, which in turn surges towards the water of Mergellina, of Via Caracciolo, of Via Partenope, of Santa Lucia, of Via Marittima, of San Giovanni a Teduccio. It would start to feel like a siege, if we didn't all know that in the end it isn't the first time it has rained like this. No, Naples has endured other rains, rains that were still more violent, yes sir. Which lasted longer. It pays its kickback, the city does, and it survives. Now there is nothing more than a sad awareness: from Via Foria the slow procession begins to quiver, and then to move. There are black cars, vans, umbrellas and these black clothes.

The father of Rosaria De Filippis is there, the first one behind that coach and eight. He would have liked the others to see her too, that day, his little girl dressed in white and with flowers in her hand, between the fingers now clamped shut. He would have liked everyone to notice the black horses from a distance, and the black coachman, and the black gravediggers, and that black coach. And inside that black the white flower of his Rosaria laid to rest with her face calm and smiling, because her father was following her. Instead they had said no, that the coffin couldn't stay open on the journey, even though he clearly remembered, he had spent the whole night in that room, and he had patiently waited for Rosaria's mother and the other ladies to take off that pair of ripped jeans and the purple sweater, and dress her, too, in that beautiful, beautiful bright white figure-hugging evening dress. And she was very elegant, his little girl, the most elegant of all. He had also told his wife, after the girl had been dressed, please put a bit of make-up on her, just just just a little bit. A seventeen-year-old girl has the right to her tender femininity, to her pretty ways, to the admiration of those who gaze upon her. Now following that coach and eight, Luigi De Filippis from time to time brought his left hand to the outside pocket of his jacket and with his fingertips gently touched and touched again to be sure: in his pocket he had kept Rosaria's glasses. Only the frame in fact which had been recovered, and through the fabric he could now discern the marks of the metal. And when they said no, that the coffin must not be open, a red violence had darted through his arms and his brain, he thought I'm going to punch them right in the face, and his muscles had tensed, his eyes narrowed with hatred, the fingers of his right hand clenched into a fist, and then, all of a sudden, the strength had gone, and the rebelliousness, and the violence, and what remained was that tender feeling, and the half-smile, and consciousness, and a relaxed expression that he couldn't see, and Rosaria's nose that shaped her delicate profile. All night he had stayed and watched: and how beautiful you are, how beautiful you are, he had gone on saying to her all that night, sitting calmly and peacefully in a chair beside the bed. Every now and again he adjusted the folds of her dress. He had never touched her face, not that, because you never touch a woman on the face, because of the make-up and the hair and the eyeliner. And all that night he had sat peacefully in the silence of his devastated house, and had said nothing but every now and then how beautiful you are, how beautiful you are, and he had really said it under his breath, in a frail hint of a voice, confiding a secret. Because he was jealous at that moment, yes, jealous, and those were facts that other people must not hear, no one must hear them, those were matters between him and his little girl, his Rosaria, and all night he had stayed on that white chair, and only at the first light of dawn – 25 October, the third day of rain – had he got up, and felt his weak knees, and his weak legs, and shaken his head for a moment, for just a moment, and then he had crossed the house, his poor devastated house, with people and flowers and some unrecognisable things, and he had gone out to stand on the balcony. He had looked up into the sky at the falling rain. He had also thought: when we leave the house the sun will be shining. Of course, the sun will be there for my Rosaria, and we will go with her with the sun and so much light around, and everyone will see her, and it will be clear that she is the most beautiful of all, my poor little girl. Now that he was following the coach in front of his nose sighed deeply with sadness, but it doesn't matter, it doesn't matter, he said to himself, because he knew very well that his little girl was the most beautiful of all, and perhaps there was really no need for the others to see her. He had felt on his right arm his wife's arm, and he had shaken off her weight, and clumsily, and he didn't want anyone's hands on him, and he didn't want anyone in front of him or beside him at that moment, because in any case nothing else mattered, what mattered was the two of them, he and his little girl, and there was no need for anything, really anything, his little girl would have imagined him coming with her. Just as he had thought of adjusting her dress when the moment had come that morning, when they had said to him you need to close it, really, you need to close it up now, and he had asked what do you mean?, close it up?, how do you close up a seventeen-year-old girl? And who will tell her about this blossoming sky and that sun that might return?, who will woo her and who will send her flowers if you close her up now? And what will that girl's life be like if now this hateful, heavy wood descends on the paleness of her face, on the tenderness of her features? After that clumsy gesture, Luigi De Filippis's wife had understood, and had fallen back a little and off to the side, because the relationship between a father and a daughter is slightly different, and men can be so strange, because they might keep things inside for years and years, and don't show anything, and then guess what. She had stepped to the left and fallen back a little and linked arms with their son, and had seen: between father and son not even a word, no, not even a word. And now the most total void had grown around Rosaria, and he alone had stayed calm, he alone, and he had wanted no one, and there had been that separation, yes, it had happened, there was no point in hiding it. He had stayed with Rosaria, and she with their son whose arm she had taken and gripped and in the course of the night she had often come to stroke without a word.

And there was that big crowd which when you were in it seemed like the whole city united all because of those seven deaths. But if you looked carefully you could see those divisions, of course, those divisions: in fact everyone had their own dead, and as regards the onlookers, well, they were broadly inclined towards the family of Aniello Savastano, not least, obviously enough, because of the three little children. Because there is always a big difference between the death of an adult and the death of a little child. The little children are redeemed, so to speak. So, near the hearses that accompanied Aniello Savastano, Aniello Savastano's wife and their three children, there were more people than there were near the coach of Rosaria De Filippis, or the hearse of Wanda Zampino, who was the old lady who had also died in the chasm. And there was that swarm of people in Via Foria, and the rumour circulated that the Higher Urban Authorities were going to come, and a speech would be delivered, but in fact now no need was felt for such a thing, for such a speech, not least because a speech had already been delivered by His Eminence the Cardinal. When a cardinal has spoken of death, what remains to be said? Perhaps something remained, something about the living, or about responsibilities, or about yet other matters, but who feels like breaking the decorum of death? Grief needs silence and rationality, and respect for the feelings of others, and it can't be done, so it can't be done. Faced with the sorrowful event, there are no objections, not a single objection.

And precisely by virtue of that fact, Giovannella Speranza had told them at home. Look I'm going to be late today, because the whole school is going to Rosaria De Filippis's funeral, and it won't be that much fun but we have to go. Her mother had looked at her and seen that her daughter's eyes were evasive, but what do you do in such difficult situations?, reply, and then Giovannella had run out in a blue skirt, her white blouse, a blue jumper and her coat on top, and soon she had reached the street, and she had turned the corner, and disappeared, she had disappeared irrevocably. On the corner behind her street she had found him closed up and closed away in the Fiat 500, and the Fiat 500, from Via Lepanto, had reached Piazzale Tecchio and then on to

Via Domitiana all the way to Damiani and beyond and when there's that sign that says Cuma to the left via that little-frequented road. At last they arrived: it was 10.15 on 25 October, the third day of rain. They got out of the Fiat 500 together with a tender kiss on the lips, and he walked ahead and showed the way, even though she knew it well, and in through the entrance immediately on the left, in that dark doorway, and then the key that is difficult to turn and then turns. They went inside, and he looked around, slightly worried, because he shared the place with someone else and wouldn't have wanted to find inconsiderate traces or anything out of place. But in the end it all went well, all well. Then he smiled and pulled the door closed behind him, while she had taken a tour, as you might say, and poked her head into the bathroom and the kitchen, after all you know what women are like, and there was a strong smell of stuffiness and also of damp, beside the bed two empty bottles, cigarette butts, and Giovannella immediately went to check, were the cigarettes hers from last time, nothing to take exception to. He watched her movements and said are we carrying out an inspection, is that it? Of course, Giovannella replied, and he smiled with that tender face of his, so tender, and he threw his arms around her neck and a deep kiss he gave her, rubbing himself against her and going MMMMM and suddenly he switched position and his hands slipped along Giovannella's hips. He felt her soft flesh under his hands, so soft, and immediately he felt a growing presence in his trousers. And also she was rubbing herself of course, and thrusting those hips forward and that tender outrageous belly, then let's put on a bit of music she said pulling suddenly away, and he was left standing in the middle of the room watching her while those little hands of hers explored and explored the radio, and found music in the end, and languidly brighter turned towards him, fumbling with her bra as he sat on the edge of the bed and leaning slightly to the side slipped his hands down below. Down below she was hot tenderly hot. In the end there was a great fuss as they tried to liberate themselves from all those clothes, and he was responsible for most of the fuss, because women are much calmer and more practical. At any rate, in the end they were naked on the bed and in a close embrace, and he kissed her, and she opened that mouth of hers a little too wide as happens sometimes when you sigh slightly, but their breath rose panting in their chests and the muscles in their arms and in their legs were now inclined to draw together. He stroked her breasts and between her legs, and she didn't stroke anything, apart from his hair, and she brought one hand down and that hand remained quite still because she had to play the part of the girl, the part of the woman. And even in fact when he climbed on top of her, Giovannella kept her legs tenderly closed tightly and they opened only when he opened them, and she went on lying underneath him. And in the end they met and, there, there, the strange sensation, strange sweetest thing in his possession coming inside and her face growing serious, and her lips parting and her eyes going blank, now, now, at that very moment that she is feeling, yes, and that movement of the loins, and the blood running now, and that strange force, and instinctively her hips move, slightly, with a brief and imperceptible movement, and he thinks for a moment and stops where he is and thinks and sees his face hidden in hers, and he is aware of their breathing and the force of those tensed muscles, and he clutches her, he clutches her so violently it hurts. And it's over, now, it's all over. Slowly, that cloudlet darkens in the distance. He stays on top of her, for a while, he kisses her tenderly on the lips. Giovannella feels from underneath that she would like to move and tremble slightly, but she can't with that cumbersome weight on top of her, and lie there she does until he comes out and doesn't turn over, and breathes deeply, of course, and smiles, and jumps up to look for a cigarette in his trousers. Giovannella says for me too. And those two cigarettes are lit. There is the sound of the rain falling, outside, methodical neurasthenic rain falling. She pulls the covers over herself and they lie there: he smoking, she thinking of her mother's eyes. She has worked it out, of course, she has worked out very clearly that she wasn't going to a funeral. Perhaps a woman who's a daughter can't lie to a woman who's a mother. But in the end it's better that she, her mother, realises, because in any case it was the same for her, and nothing to make a song and dance about, no. They all know very well that at a certain age girls open their legs and make love. She did the same, when the time came. So why does she go on at her like that, why? He lies there smoking with his eyes fixed on the ceiling. Giovannella gives him a kick. He lifts himself up on his elbow towards her breasts and rests his lips tenderly on them and for a while they joke and talk about themselves and other people and there's always lots to talk about. When he approaches again and rubs against her thigh, Giovannella becomes aware of that hard presence, and now it starts again, she says to herself, and indeed it does start again, and this time better, much better. When the movement comes Giovannella stretches into her loins and grips grips with her legs in an arc holding on, and that river that comes oh that river and the world opening up and the earth opening up, now, and she receives, yes, she receives it all, the furrow comes down, down into the depths, oh yes, and that river that is a whole sea now, a wide enormous boundless sea, and there is this open air, and this pace and her heart swells, and those arms leaving me, and those legs leaving me and those hands that have abandoned me oh yes abandoned oh yes abandoned. Then slowly conscious thought returns, she says, damn! She grips him, she plants a kiss on him, and then she looks at the clock. Of course, the clock: there's not much to joke about, at home. Seven days before, then she was late, her father gave her two slaps that she can still feel on her face. Giovannella Speranza decides that it really isn't a good idea to make the situation worse, and that there are ways and ways of doing things. A woman if she is a woman always finds the right way. And she doesn't need to look her in the eyes, her mother doesn't, with that falsely apprehensive expression as if she could understand who knows what. There, you see, mamma?, here I am completely naked in bed and nothing is happening, really nothing at all. If I think about the way you used to fuss in the old days, the way you want to fuss again, it just makes me laugh thinking about it. And the worries that I carried with me, and the gossip of my friends, and those dark questions, and that thing that weighed so heavily. And too bad that I've sorted it out, too bad, if it had been up to you I would have had to drag it around with me for another ten years, wouldn't I?, just ten, and then maybe all those other things about marriage and life. My dears, the more time passes, the more I realise, with the best will in the world, that there's very little in all the things you say, yes, very little, because when I move in my own way I see everything differently, and things are never the same as you told me they were, and as you would like to go on telling me they are, never the same, never, not even once. Then really you would wonder if you weren't in another world. Maybe you haven't noticed and in the meantime the world has shifted, it's moved a little further on, and you haven't noticed, you're still twisting your things thingies thingummies around in your hands and in the meantime everything has changed, of course, everything, and what has not changed is about to change, without a doubt. If I think again of that thing that I carried around with me, if I think about it. But anyway, now, let's see if we can start moving because it's getting late. Outside in the street it was raining harder now. That strip of grey in the sky, everything seemed heavier. Giovannella Speranza, there, now, became aware of her separation from him: he was certainly steering off somewhere else. He had set off on a different route, somewhere far away.

Just so, at that moment, did Rosaria De Filippis, Wanda Zampino and Aniello Savastano with his family turn into a different road, very far away, and the crowd dispersed into a hundred tiny trickles, and in the end only the groups of family and relatives had remained, in the cemetery of Poggioreale. Each group had seen the other making for a different destination, and the solidarity of death had shattered silently now because of those partings, and in the end each one of them was left with their own dead, and perhaps because of that dispersal they felt diminished, as if life had stolen something from them. Certainly, compared with two hours previously, the atmosphere was completely different, and that participation, and the multitude of voices, and the quiet murmur had made them forget even the falling rain, everything had been set aside, two hours before: the little torrents of water along the sides of the road, the overflowing sewers gurgling water, and those streams of water that were on the way, and the silence that had been there as a clue. While now that presence of rain drew on the alleyways of Poggioreale, and the water came down the hill, and everyone was sure that it had nothing to do with them, nothing at all. The water came down came down fled into the distance, and somewhere it would stop too, in all likelihood, but that didn't concern any of them, no: it only concerned those who were in the place where the water stopped: but, in the end: would it ever really stop, that water that kept coming and coming? And even if it did, what would ever happen? There was only that grey presence to disrupt their thoughts, to confuse their eyes.

And it was the third day of rain, 25 October.

At about 7pm, in the courtyard of the Maschio Angioino, the cars began to arrive. They came with that faint sound of windscreen wipers, tic tac tic tac tic tac, and as they passed the police cordon the police brought their hands to their berets and saluted. Nothing survived in the courtyard but that arrangement of cars parked at an angle so that the exit could be reached. But: would there ever be an exit?, would this session ever end? Would the Baronial Hall not be turned, that evening, into an enormous trap?

Perhaps columns of peasants with scythes and pitchforks would come running from the countryside. They would invade the courtyard, disrupting the police cordon. Shouting they would climb the stone stairs and would burst into the reddish electric light of the hall, with big boots on their feet, kerchiefs around the necks, their arms brawny, and they would begin a cruel manhunt. The municipal councillors would attempt an impossible escape across the wooden benches, with those shouts and that heavy breathing behind them, and they would feel themselves being gripped by the legs and the arms, and they would open their mouths as they attempted to speak. Shut up!, the others would yell at them instead, traitor to the people! Two three four pitchforks would run through their chests, and they would feel the blades in their flesh and they would scream, scream, and streams of blood would gush from their flabby flesh and spill down they would in the end lie lifeless on the ground. The peasants would work doggedly with their scythes. Get the head, get the head!, they would hear them cry. Five six seven arms would get to work with the scythes to part their heads from their necks. It isn't as easy as you think to detach a head from the neck, it doesn't just come off like that, oh no. It remains attached with muscles and bones and there's just that flowing blood on all sides. You have to strike resolutely and with full force. After twenty blows at last the head really comes off. The heads would be slipped on to long poles and, then, exposed on the crenellated bastions in that flaming night. Cries of jubilation would rise into the night, and everything would be destroyed, and the benches of the council building would go up in an enormous bonfire, and high the flames would rise to illuminate from a distance that tormented city. And gone in the end would be the crowds of peasants, swarming through the deserted rain-thrashed city. The fire would last until the first light of dawn with the acrid smell of smoke, and that silent crackle. And that rain falling, interminably.

When the hall was full enough, and quiet confabulations could be heard in the corridors, it was decided that it was time to begin the session. The Mayor said I declare the session of the municipal council open, first of all the agenda: extraordinary interventions for childcare facilities. And Mr Mayor, said a councillor, I think that the foremost task of the council is to deal with the tragic event of Aniello Falcone and the tragic event of Via Tasso, it is unimaginable on the part of anyone etcetera etcetera. And then it became immediately clear to the gentlemen of the majority party that they would not have an easy ride of it that evening, and that even the most probing eyes were watching with concern: the space reserved for the public was fast being filled, and other people were still bound to arrive, and there would be protests. The Mayor said certainly certainly, and called over Antonino Sale, not yet a councillor, he hadn't quite made it that time, but he was still a capable pair of hands, and in short when it came to the crunch there was no one more suited than he. He said come and gauge the mood on that side. Because we are very much disposed to deal with the tragic event and we also realise: the opposition will inevitably cause trouble, if only to show all those people that the opposition's hands are clean and that they are performing their acknowledged functions of criticism and crack-papering, and all of those fine things. We are very well aware. So let them cause as much trouble as they wish, but take care not to overstate their case. Because if they come down too hard, the agreement on the professional course to be taken is blown away, blown away once and for all. In short, my dear Antonino Sale, off you go on a reconnaissance mission and see how we're going to get these issues across. Antonino Sale casually went to chat to this person and that. Meanwhile, the council member for the opposition said: it certainly isn't the first time that our wretched city has had to record such tragic events, just as it isn't the first time that adverse atmospheric conditions have determined situations of alarm or at least of alert, but we must obviously continue to ask ourselves, fellow councillors, what were, technically speaking, the causes of these upheavals, and whether those causes might be attributable to chance, to accident, to the whims of fate, or whether they should not rather be attributed to neglect, to slothfulness and incompetence, as well as to fact that works and repairs and the reconstruction of the sewerage system which everyone had identified for years as urgent and pressing had been put off indefinitely. We may obviously wonder, gentlemen, whether the tragic events with which the council at present has a civil and above all a moral obligation to address constitute the extreme conclusion of exceptional and therefore unpredictable events, or whether those events are not in fact that logical conclusion of a series of administrative shortcomings all of which may be traced back to the incompleteness and inadequacy of a governance of the public good whose role it is to address uniquely illuminating events, such as that of the gold incinerator, to take one example, and which instead disregards that possibly awkward and perhaps not well-remunerated administrative sector which holds responsibilities with regard to road conditions, the clearing of rain water, the channelling of the same, and to get to the nub, gentlemen, let it be pointed out straight away that the relevant councillor, or indeed the Mayor himself if he considers it appropriate, will be doing something most welcome if he explains to the council how it is possible that after an impressive amount of works, which amongst other things for a good two years have kept entirely closed and blocked that important urban artery which goes by the name of Via Tasso, three days of not particularly violent rain were enough to cause a sinkhole of the dimensions of the one that has just appeared. While this councillor was delivering his speech, a murmur rose up among the crowd. They were asking the name of the councillor in question, and which party he belonged to. Meanwhile, his leader had already gestured to him to come forward, to continue the speech, and in fact the councillor, who knew how to speak discreetly, came forward straight away, listing the faults and shortcomings of the civic administration, not only and not so much with regard to the tragic event of recent days, but not least and above all with regard to the general state of neglect and uncertainty which afflicts, and not only since today, all of the city's structures and substructures. And in fact the councillor, for the sake of coming forward, came forward, except that a mounting sense of embarrassment took hold of him as he followed with his eyes the secret discussion that was at that very moment going on between the head of the Majority and the head of the Opposition. And bearing in mind that point of visible reference the councillor continued with his speech, stressing how the tragic event had once again provided dramatic evidence of the inadequacy and superficiality of the public intervention in the area, etcetera etcetera. And the head of the Opposition, having concluded his lengthy secret discussion with the head of the Majority, approached him discreetly and, still with extreme discretion, whispered: we are requesting a commission of inquiry. Then the councillor went on saying it is precisely with a view to overcoming such shortcomings, such confusions, such reprehensible defects, Mr Mayor, that we are putting forward an operational proposal: that is the formation and appointment of a commission of inquiry with the precise mandate to make every useful attempt to ascertain responsibility, should such responsibilities exist, and establish why and in what way Naples must pay such a high annual tribute in terms of human lives because of adverse atmospheric conditions which cannot be described as unpredictable or to be on the scale of an exceptional event or a cataclysm, because let it be quite clear to everyone that, if the dead cannot do it, the living demand justice, and we must not in any way excuse ourselves from that precise civil and above all moral obligation. When the councillor had concluded his speech, followed distractedly in the hall but carefully savoured by the public, the journalists exchanged meaningful glances from the press benches. In short, it was clear that the Opposition had made this speech solely and exclusively for reasons of honour, that in fact they had been careful not to cause too much trouble. And on the other hand that was largely predictable, if one were to bear in mind that there had been that morning a joint meeting concerning the use of the new funds made available by the Region for the maintenance of professional training courses, and if we bear in mind that those funds amounted to one billion eight hundred million lire. Now that the speech was completed, the Mayor said that the Majority adopted the proposal put forward by the Opposition and then decided to proceed to the constitution and to the appointment of a commission of inquiry in which all parties would be represented, with the purpose and the declared objective of casting a full light on the tragic events of Via Aniello Falcone and Via Tasso and to ascertain who might or might not bear responsibility, and if necessary the commission itself would be able to seek advice from a shortlist of officially appointed experts. The Municipality of Naples paid dutiful homage to the victims of the disaster. Everyone rose to their feet, and even among the public the murmurs stopped immediately, and everyone stood silently like that, and some people began to wonder how long a minute's silence really was and in fact only fifteen seconds had passed when murmuring to himself the Mayor sat down again. Then everyone sat down again, and even the public resumed its conversation. In short, it was possible to trace everything back to an orderly pursuance of roadworks. The subsequent speeches had the same calm and reasonable tone as usual. A council meeting is not a rally, a street demonstration, and its purpose is certainly not to satisfy the base instincts of the so-called masses. The council is in fact the worthy seat, both worthy and opportune, for the peaceful debate of the problems of the city, for the solution of which, for the best possible solution of which, both sides must make their own effective contribution. And in short it was now more than clear to the public that there was nothing amusing going on here, far from it. Because there was no fascinating, riveting rhetorical duel in the offing, no argument about to set the session alight, and no one going to strike the bench with his fist and shout that's enough now! The speeches had been so calm and reasonable that the sound in the hall was not only and not so much one of composed voices as it was the cold and in many respects cruel hiss of the rain outside, leaving greyish vertical stripes on the black of the night. In the courtyard, the waiting cars waited with waiting drivers waiting. And the police had taken shelter under the portico, because in the end a police cordon is a great bore, which you can man without getting soaked to the skin. In the darkness of that night, which was the third night of uninterrupted rain, the glow of cigarettes shone from time to time with puffs of smoke fringed by the rain. And it was as if during those hours an incomplete and distorted question had risen over the silent city, just a hypothesis, the idea of a question. A question that refused to emerge, that refused to emerge at all, which everyone sensed deep in the tissue between rib and rib. As they breathed, they became aware of its concrete presence in the diaphragm. Over the city that dark presence, and with it fear, and foreboding as well: now perhaps the perspective on life would change, oh, yes, be changed and disrupted for ever. There would be an adjustment, a strange conversion. Inside the chasm that had appeared on Via Aniello Falcone the rain was now coming down with an unusually determined violence. Just as it was thundering ruthlessly down on the overflowing sewers on Via Tasso. That water was fleeing quickly towards the sea along the other different ancient streets of the city, and alarms were going off increasingly, and those voices in the thick night were made of magma, harsh and concerned. During the night of that third day of rain, reliable witnesses state that they saw cars slipping silently on the grey of the tarmac with white lights, with red lights, with blue lights, and without sirens, without breaking the silence, and those cars slipped silently along the streets of the promenade. From the red brick pyramid where they climbed to dispute one another's right of way, and sprays of spume, and that salty smell, that moving water, moving lightly in some ways, which was rising up against the black of night to meet the rain coming down, and that darkness around it. Black darkness, still and silent. One wondered if it would be wise to leave, oh yes, to leave. And why not?, for what specific reason? To gather things together in silence, to close everything up, close it up and lock it up and protect and gauge and assess with a swift glance, and climb inside one's car, and set it in motion, turn on the lights, reach the motorway. From the motorway off you went forever, of course, as definitively as a full stop, a decision both irrevocable and unamenable to reassessment in the cold light of day. Away from the city in the depths of night, as far away as a separation, scorched earth, that's it, a clean break. And it also needed to be borne in mind that the rising of the sea level at Montedidio had occurred that summer. Not without reason, certainly. In fact it was all clear. As a harbinger, a warning. And even though in that moment they might have thought and conjectured about who-knows-what unusual tidal phenomenon, now, in the light of that rain and that difficult question, everything was clear, yes. Everyone remembered the morning of Sunday 5 August, and as they remembered it was like touching revealed truth, and illumination dilated the pupil. Born of a flash of inspiration it now proceeded along the road to consciousness.

*

Because in fact on the morning of Sunday 5 August not only had the police and their vehicles taken up strategic positions on the promenade, there had also been reinforcements and senior officers from the Carabinieri, as well as the regular police. The patrols had taken solid possession of the beach at Mergellina, the Diaz Memorial, the Broken Column on Piazza Vittoria, Molosiglio, Santa Lucia, and at each point a patrol had launched the operation which would go down in the annals of the city as Operation Sea Watch. In fact they had been talking about it for some time that summer, about the operation hastily drawn up by the forces of law and order. The episode had filled the pages of the newspapers and had passed from mouth to mouth and story to story until it had been completely distorted, but in any case on this occasion the news pages were still the most reliable sections of the daily newspapers. In short, on the morning of Sunday 5 August, it had been clear, extremely clear, to all the ragged boys on the promenade, and it had been equally clear to their big sisters and to their fat, shuffling mothers, that it would be impossible to reach the rocks that day, and it would therefore be impossible for them to throw themselves into the sea, and bask in the sun. And whatever ingenious schemes the ragged children came up with on the spot, really on the spot, the situation appeared tactically impossible. Because of the fact that the deployment of the forces of law and order was genuinely impressive: hundreds and hundreds of men all firmly guarding the key points and keeping the surviving points under surveillance with regular patrols. At the first signs, darting away in one direction and then switching back to another at great speed, the ragged boys of the promenade tried to penetrate the lines of the guards. But penetration was impossible. Two or three large hands would inevitably grab them by the hair, it was painful to be pulled by the hair like that, and there were these cries from the boys every now and again. But after a few minutes they were released into the most pointless freedom, after a few minutes, having learned that from that day forward in Naples they could not go swimming, and they could not go on the rocks, or take the sun, or dive into the water. So groups formed in the shadow of the Villa Comunale, and on the pavement in front of it. It was ten o'clock in the morning on the morning of Sunday 5 August. The boys thought it was just a matter of waiting, that sooner or later the guards would leave, the promenade would be clear again, if they waited briefly and patiently everything would be resolved. Then they began that slight invisible siege on the shadow of the Villa Comunale. And their eyes darted every now and again in the direction of the sea. The sea was under guard, truly under guard. Along the horizon, those dark uniforms, the jeeps, the blue cars of the police with the white letters Comune di Napoli. The minutes filtered through the leaves of the trees. That presence of the sun. Completely white, in the distance. The blue of the sea also blurred into white. And how hard and long was that slight and invisible siege. At about 1pm it was clear to everyone, even to those who had left temporarily to return to the battlefield: the blue uniforms would not be moving from there all day, no, they weren't about to move for anything. And besides, never had the instructions of their superiors been more precise and categorical than they were on this occasion. Precise and categorical both as regards the places – the whole promenade of the city, from Mergellina to Molosiglio, was to be placed under guard – and the period during which it was to be effective – the guard was to last until half an hour after sunset, and while sunset might in itself be an arguable concept, the precise intention of the arrangements was clear to all those deployed to enforce it. At about 1pm the boys of Naples were obliged to accept, with some bitterness, that the blue uniforms were going to stay in place, and that they would not be moving for the rest of the day. Then that barrier became a barrier of hatred, and of mute rancour. Because the sea belongs to everyone without distinction. It is beyond imagining that one day the authorities will wake up and arrange themselves here and here, depriving the boys of the sea, and there was no point trying to explain to the shuffling and bundled mothers that the Municipality had permitted free bathing in some establishments in Posillipo, because in fact the boys of Montedidio really had no desire to go to Posillipo. For years and for generations the boys had bathed, always for the whole of those long, long Neapolitan summers, in those waters right in front of them, in that sea which was their sea, on those rocks which were their rocks, and why change all of a sudden the prospect of something rooted in the natural order of things?, for what unfamiliar reason?, for what capricious whim? It was at around one o'clock that a painful awareness made itself felt, and the ragged children climbed back up towards the city abandoning the Villa Comunale and abandoning the Gardens of Molosiglio. It would have to be said that there was a great deal of sadness, in that grim slog homewards, really a great deal of sadness. For a day the whole city had that veil over its eyes, the mild and melancholy air.

On receipt of the calm and peaceful news via radio, the authorities sighed deeply with relief and their faces settled into a half-smile: in fact, on the eve of Operation Sea Watch, there had been many doubts and intense discussions. It had even been feared that the operation might not go smoothly, indeed that there might be incidents and disorder. You know what schemers are like, always ready to take advantage of the slightest opportunity for attrition, and in short, on the eve, everyone had said let's hope it goes well, and now that it was after one and the boys had sadly climbed back up to Montedidio, abandoning their outpost of the Villa Comunale and Molosiglio, it seemed that all had turned out for the best. Nothing could disturb that calm, serene air that breathed warmly now on the city's promenade. And there was this air of resignation on the one hand, and of regained calm serenity on the other.

And it was precisely in consideration of the fact that the situation was firmly and definitively under control, that Ferdinando De Rosa, Marshal of the Carabinieri, said fine, rummaged in his pockets, took out a pack of cigarettes and lit one, drawing on it violently and with relief. Inhaling the smoke, he looked at the sea right in front of him, and there was this horizontal strip, the profile of Vesuvius, of Punta della Campanella, of the Isle of Capri. The sun bleached everything white. There were many boats on the water. He stood like that watching until he noticed that the sea seemed to be coming towards him. The first time he noticed he said to himself that's impossible, that's absolutely impossible. Or perhaps it is possible, what do I know about the sea? And in fact Ferdinando De Rosa reflected that he was profoundly ignorant about every aspect of the sea. Yes, there had been that thing about tides that come and go, which he had studied at school many years before, but apart from that he had never taken the slightest interest in the sea, not least and principally because of the fact that his wife's illnesses, all nervous in origin, had repeatedly obliged them to take holidays, with the children the aunt and everybody, in the area around Lake Laceno, where they were all fine and entirely heedless of the disastrous effects of the sea on the nervous systems of people who suffered with their nerves. Because of that age-old habit he had gradually lost all contact with the sea. He had been left with a vague feeling of the time when he was a boy and sailing at school and he and his friends hired a rowing boat from the fishermen of Mergellina, and it was therefore a matter of rowing and rowing for hours under the sun. There were no bathing costumes in those days, there was nothing at all, those boys rowed cheerfully until they reached the open sea, and in the end with the heat and the sweat there was nothing for it but to strip off completely and throw themselves into the water. Every time he remembered that day, he inevitably also remembered a thin boy with glasses, no idea what his name was. He never wanted to get completely naked, so he swam in his very big white underpants which hung down because of the bony thinness of his legs and hips. He also remembered that if you lowered your head from the boat and stared at the sea it was as if you had gone to sleep. From below you couldn't see anything but the slow movement of the water, the green and the azure blue, an unchanging stillness, an infinite variation of tones and colours. In the end the sunlight etched itself on his retinas. And in fact that was what he knew about the sun. Apart from jellyfish, which he had sometimes seen from the boat, and one of them had come very close to him, really close, while he was swimming in the water, but in the end nothing had happened that time, because calmly and keeping an eye on the jellyfish he had got back to the boat, he had hauled himself up on his arms and gone on staring at the water of the sea, strange, curious, transparent creature. Otherwise, he knew nothing about the sea. Ferdinando De Rosa had suddenly been very clear after getting married: Patrizia was sick with her nerves. The sea wasn't really the reason, not at all, the fat doctor from the National Health had told him, but anyway she needed to holiday in a cool place in the countryside, in the hills if possible. In fact he was already aware by around the month of April, when it first turned warm, that Patrizia really couldn't bear the heat, and at night she wandered the length the house and back again, and she couldn't sleep, and in the morning she wore a face, hollow-eyed and shattered, as if she had done something in the course of the night, when in fact she hadn't done anything at all. Sometimes he had surprised her in the early afternoon talking to herself on the terrace at home. At such moments he felt a pang in his heart, seeing her like that. Then he came slowly up behind her and gave her a kiss on the back of the neck, a kiss on the cheek, she smiled weakly as if to say thank you, yes exactly as if she was saying thank you, but in fact he was very clearly aware: Patrizia was far away, so far away. At that moment, and in the previous moments on that precise day, and on the previous days, she seemed sometimes to take refuge in that little corner that was all her own and withdraw from everything. It was because of Patrizia's nervous frailty that in the end they had to call her aunt to ask if she couldn't come and stay with them for a little while. Not so much to look after the house or the children, not that, so much as to keep Patrizia company for all the time that he was out on duty, and to check that her nervous fragility did not lead to anything serious, because who could guess the thoughts of a woman who was sick with nerves who was left at home alone with her children? Then the aunt had come to the house, and from the very first for Ferdinando De Rosa everything was immediately clear, oh yes: their life as a couple was shattered, shattered forever. But in any case there was nothing else to do, nothing else to do but keep a constant eye on Patrizia, and with those watches that they were doing at Gruppo Napoli II there wasn't much to be cheerful about. He was particularly aware that with those watches he no longer had any time of his own. In fact some evenings he was tired, really tired and he came home and he saw his wife, and the children, and the aunt, and very often also Patrizia's mother, a fat and unbearable woman who looked at him askance as if it was his fault that Patrizia had ended up in that state, as if it was because of the marriage, or perhaps the children he had given her, that her little Patrizia had ended up with that fragility of the nerves which meant that now she couldn't even be left on her own, because her mother was afraid of something and everyone was really afraid of something, even if nothing ever happened, but how could you run the risk of something happening?, who would have assumed responsibility if something anomalous and terrible had happened all of a sudden? In short it had been for these remarkable reasons that he in one respect or another had never had anything to do with the sea, and every time he remembered the sea Ferdinando De

Rosa remembered the boat trip with his friends, and the jellyfish, and not many other things.

So when he had the impression, that morning, that the sea had grown, and that it had risen slightly, he was left with those doubts of his and the awareness of his own ignorance about the sea. He found himself thinking that perhaps he hadn't seen properly, and that perhaps even if the sea had risen a little, it meant nothing but the recurrent play of the tides. He had studied at school but he didn't really remember it now. Certainly there was a tide that rose and a tide that fell, and that was also bound up with the alternation of day and night, but in fact however many attempts he made he couldn't really remember anything, he remembered only that vague thing and it wasn't enough, it wasn't enough at all. When he noticed for the first time, on that Sunday morning, 4 August, that the sea had grown, he stood in silence reflecting and waiting calmly and patiently. Besides, the sea was always the same placid sea, nothing to worry about in any respect, nothing that could cause anxious thoughts. The boats went as they always went, and on the parapet of Santa Lucia he had the good sense to make a mark so as to check the water level in future. So he made that visible mark and let a few minutes pass. As the time passed, letting the time pass, he felt something within him like a dark foreboding, a worry that was unjustified but vivid and real. Besides, his worry was broadly justified by what happened next, a few minutes later, when checking the mark he had made he noticed for the second time, this time without any doubt whatsoever: the sea had risen again. And in itself this would not have mattered in the slightest had it not been for the mounting sense of foreboding which seemed to provide an interpretation of everything which aroused remote and indistinguishable fears. Ferdinando De Rosa now reflected that he might have been mistaken, insofar as this rising of the sea constituted a ritually composed and regular event, but in any case henceforth it was his duty to be mistaken in company and not only on his own. It was in consideration of such reflections that he also showed the other carabinieri in what way and to what extent the sea had now been rising for some minutes at that spot. At first a deep sense of dismay took hold of the militiamen, not least because it is difficult for any carabiniere, however expert, to stop the sea, or proceed to its identification, and you can't take the sea by the arm or if called upon to do so use handcuffs, so this state of dull embarrassment prevailed for some time. On the other hand everyone found themselves thinking, Ferdinando De Rosa and all the others; if it is true on the one hand that this strange, unusual and alarming phenomenon may occur, it is also true on the other hand that nothing, nothing at all, on that morning of Sunday 5 August, gave any clue to any inauspicious or tragic events, and in any case the situation seemed to be under control, yes, even with the sea rising like that. Of course the best resolution, subject to later checks, was to alert the superiors, inform those who, being of higher rank, also indubitably had the task of solving problems and assuming certain responsibilities, and obviously that decision was not to be taken on the spur of the moment, certainly not, because there was still a fear of making a poor impression on one's superiors. But it would also have to be said that in the meantime on the round terrace of Mergellina there was a murmur of fishermen who had seen the sea rising and couldn't figure it out, because in the course of their lives they had seen all manner of things but they had quite definitely never seen the sea rising with that Olympian calm, that joyful, almost laughing serenity of rising waves. Because in fact, even though the sea was clearly rising no one could really find it in themselves to worry about it. The sea wasn't swelling and it wasn't getting dark and it didn't seem to be threatening anything, and in the end it was a sea that was still clearly a friend, a friend to fisherfolk and people on boating trips, the same calm, familiar sea as ever, nothing at all that might raise anxieties or dark forebodings. Aside from that extremely concrete awareness of the unignorable fact that the sea, beyond any doubt, had begun to rise. Yes, it had begun to rise and seemed to be continuing to do so. The same carabinieri, on the wall at Santa Lucia, at last agreed that there was nothing to be done but to alert the superiors, and radio contact was therefore established with the headquarters of Gruppo Napoli II. In the meantime, the water level had reached the parapet, and from one minute to the next the sea was going to overflow on to the pavement and into the road, yes, it was going to overflow. That fateful moment came at last and it came at the very moment when the police instruction came from Napoli II headquarters that they were not under any circumstances to abandon their position. Upon receipt of that instruction the officers immediately fell into line with a strong sense of discipline. Moreover, perhaps the wisest thing to do in these circumstances was to go on guarding that spot. And then, in any case, it became clear to everyone, even when the water overflowed from the parapet and on to the pavement, that for the time being at least there was no danger. No danger of any kind, apart from the irritation of water getting into your shoes, and sticking your trousers to your calves, and to your socks, but that was merely a matter of discomfort, of continuous embarrassment, certainly not a dangerous situation. Then the patrol went on patrolling regularly, even though the water had now filled the whole width of the pavement and spilled from the kerb on to the tarmac of the road. It was that brackish seawater that ran from one pavement to the other. It advanced in slow rivulets, and there was always that patch of water pushing forwards, pointing the way, just as seawater does when it reaches the shore, except that this time there was no backwash, the patch of seawater, that thin veil, continued on its way. From Via Partenope it climbed up Via Nazario Sauro and then to Piazza del Plebiscito, and in fact people stopped to look, and there really was something to look at, if we are to maintain a degree of objectivity. Because in reality no one had ever seen anything like it before, and neither would they in all likelihood see anything like it again in days to come, and in the end the rising sea is a very strange phenomenon. Then the people gazed down in puzzlement at the tarmac and that patch of seawater advancing, advancing, followed by all the rest of the water from the sea. And it was clear to everyone that this was not just something that was happening as the result of some dramatic or evil trick, oh no. It was clear straight away that, however unusual or supernatural the nature of this event, it too somehow fell within the natural order of things, and it had its own specific reasons, and what was being observed at that moment was therefore not a negative event, far from it. Except that obviously none of them could help thinking and reflecting on the joyful, almost laughing nature of this phenomenon, and in the end their sense of wonder was remarkable, and in many respects justified, but such considerations remained deeply alien to the strength and why not the biological determination of the seawater, which from Piazza del Plebiscito in the course of a few minutes – what time could it be?, half past one in the afternoon? – went on rising up along Via Gennaro Serra and reached Montedidio, the houses, the streets and alleyways of Montedidio, and seeped into the basements. In fact the seawater was doing nothing other than undermining the houses, one by one, patiently and meticulously, all the ragged boys who had not been able to get to the rocks on Via Partenope, on Via Caracciolo, in Mergellina that morning, and the sea saw this as a gesture of love, and in fact that is exactly what it was. Many considered with vivid alarm that a shapeless and sometimes tarry liquid mass could feed on such feelings with regard to the boys who had been unable to swim that day, but the evidence of the facts was truly blinding, it had never been more blinding. That brackish water insinuated itself everywhere, licking soft calves, touching toes. On that day, which was Sunday 5 August, it was truly clear to everyone that if the boys had not gone to the sea because they had been prevented from so doing by Operation Sea Watch, the sea, for once, had come to find the boys. It had done so with the boys' own cheerful and punctilious determination. In fact, thinking again now about that unusual event already slightly spoiled by the passing of time, thinking again now about that event on the morning of Sunday 5 August, it dawned on the mind that this had in all likelihood been an alert, a warning significant in its way, and in short the question which concerned us now was perhaps substantially the question of 5 August, or at least not dissimilar, even though then in fact they could not help noticing the latent anxiety they were feeling right now had been entirely unknown on that August day. In fact they all remembered very clearly how that August day had been a joyful and a laughing day, a holiday, while now this rain that was coming down and coming down was something much harsher and more cruel, more than anything it bent your head forcing you downwards, and the feeling had shed any connotation of gaiety, beyond any doubt. There was nothing to smile about any more, with this rain now, nothing at all in the end, and in fact the cruel harshness of a vague and heavy question was concentrating in people's fists. On the city, if you looked up, that veil of rain was coming down and coming down, and the rain marked a fine weft in the distance, and the same thoughts were damp and wrinkled thoughts, deeply marked by that fine vertical rain that was falling falling on threads of water that mingled with the fallen water and the water that was yet to fall, and because now there was a harsh and deep and cruel awareness: this rain would continue, yes, it would continue until the event became apparent, until the ultimate significance became clear and apparent even to the most defenceless and the weakest minds. In fact all that remained was to reconsider everything, really everything, from a perspective other than this one of waiting opened up by the rain. Waiting weighed on hearts like a gigantic press, fixed and inescapable, it fell with the harsh and heavy determination of continuous reproach. And that was the third day of rain. The city of Naples was so disheartened that it choked back its playful melancholic streak and folded away its florid thoughts in a dark corner of the house, along with the rubber mattress and battered fishing tackle.

*

And it was not until 7.30pm on that same day that Pasquale De Crescenzo became fully aware that no more people were going to come. Then he looked dolefully at the seats in their neat rows, the fertilised plants, the Press Club flowers, the waiters coming and going, and it was as if they always had very many things to do. But in fact he wondered what they really had to do, given that there were not more than twenty people in the room, most of them friends and family members. He wondered also, looking dolefully towards the window, if that gloomy, stubborn rain that had been steadily falling for three days and with those sad conscious thoughts would cease. And there was a strange silence in that room, because in fact everyone was very careful not to speak, and everyone was in a state of waiting, at least waiting to know how it would all end. And besides if you are talking in public, it is necessary for the public to be large, so it then covers the murmur with its own murmur, and in the end gentlemen everyone wants to have their back covered in life, it is by no means a matter of leaving yourself exposed and isolated. In general those who expose themselves always come to a bad end, and in life hardly anyone wishes to come to a bad end and even if there was someone who did wish such a thing, or did until a few days ago, now in fact with that rain that was coming down and coming down, and those distorted questions, and that unusual waiting, now no longer wished such a thing, and wished instead to participate, and to be involved in things, and therefore not to expose themselves, no, not in the slightest. In the end there was this silence, in the room, and what became apparent, along with the faint sound of the rain falling, the muted gurgle, in the little bar, of the espresso machine. Pasquale De Crescenzo said to himself that in such circumstances it would be appropriate to close the glass door dividing the hall from the bar. In fact, he believed that writing poetry was difficult enough, but that of course more difficult and tricky, in this strange city but also elsewhere in all the cities of the world, was making people listen to poetry. Because you needed an unexpected detail, that was it, the muted gurgle of the coffee machine, to distract the mind, distract it, and remove it from the verses. Because in fact Pasquale De Crescenzo had noticed on more than one occasion: life is hostile, deeply hostile to poetry. Life is something extremely concrete and tangible that does not want poetry, it can't bear it. And even with all those jokes, and all that flattery, and girls applauding, and saying oh yes oh yes, in fact things are different, he knew very well how things were. Many many times he had resisted, in the homes of friends, and had looked sadly up at the windowpanes, and from outside he had seen the night sky with all its lights. Then he reflected sadly that in all likelihood there was no point continuing with the evening as planned, and in the end it struck him as entirely pointless for Maria De Giovanni to deliver her opening introductory presentation to the lyric poems of Pasquale De Crescenzo. Above all for the extremely valid reason that there had as yet been no sign of Maria De Giovanni that evening, and she never would appear, and secondly because the poems of Pasquale De Crescenzo spoke for themselves, and there was no need for any presentation or introduction, gentlemen, because poetry is what it is, it is pleasing, if it is not pleasing on its own it is the poetry that is wrong, or perhaps you are incapable of grasping it. Having mulled these thoughts, Pasquale De Crescenzo then got to his feet resting his hands on the green tabletop, for a long time studied the bottle of mineral water and the empty bottles, the two ashtrays strategically placed in anticipation of a huge influx of people to the table of honour, he carefully studied his fingernails, the ten nails of his ten fingers, and said at last: gentlemen. I am truly sorry that adverse atmospheric conditions have kept numbers smaller than they would doubtless have been under different circumstances, but on the other hand we must take account of reality and adapt to it, you all know that this evening's programme included, before the poetry reading, an introductory presentation by Professor Maria De Giovanni, who has been prevented from taking part by difficulties with public transport, and therefore, with great regret, we will all have to do without the programmed talk and I will find myself all alone, and besides I don't really have much to say, I will tell you one thing only and I hope that you will all share my enthusiasm: the language of Ferdinando Russo and Salvatore Di Giacomo is not dead, it is alive and vital today more than ever, today and in the years to come, because the so-called vernacular is not a literary invention, an artificial construction made by experts and linguistic experimenters, but the most authentic, the most genuine and the most felt expression of an entire people, that people which, in the reign of the Bourbons, enjoyed a superior position in civil and artistic life, and from the perspective of their history went on to maintain a true individuality and singularity, inexpressible except through the purest expressions of the purest Neapolitan dialect, so, gentlemen, in the hope that it may serve some useful purpose I should like this evening to strike a blow for the defence and protection of our language. Well, considering my brief introduction is at an end, let us move on to the poetry, which may not be great poetry, it may not pass into the literary history of this great city and this country, but it most certainly constitutes concrete testimony of a love of the city, a love of Naples, which is the truly unique characteristic of all the sons of Queen Partenope, and now we have come to the poems which as you know have been collected in a volume by the publisher Cosentino Fausto under the title *Napule ca luce*, and I should like to begin this short meeting with one of the poems closest to my heart, which seems to me to be particularly indicative of the possibility of making poetry today in the Partenopean vernacular, the poem in question is entitled 'L'Ammore è 'na palomma'. Love is a Dove. So Pasquale De Crescenzo began in that faltering voice of his, and as always happened, down in the depths of his throat he became aware of a tremor in his vocal cords. But that only affected the first few lines, he knew very well, he realised that every time, that soon his voice would be coming out very smoothly, his voice would acquire pleasing and elastic inflections, and at last he began

L'Ammore è 'na palomma
ca nun vo cchiù vulà

love is a dove that no longer wishes to fly, and he became aware that inadvertently his eyes had fallen upon the twenty people present, as if personally checking their approval of a poem that was very close to his heart, but by which he was in essence not particularly convinced, in the sense that apart from the musicality of the verse it was a conceptual proposition that on more than one occasion had prompted strong doubts concerning the final and recondite significance, but why for heaven's sake recondite?, of this poetry of his. In that brief space, his eyes rose to check beyond his glasses, and he felt a sense of unease. Because those twenty people, rather than pressing together compactly in the centre in front of him were all scattered like dust around the hall, and every one of them had chosen to sit towards the back rows of chairs, and in the end the first rows, which were the ones directly in front of his eyes, were deserted, completely deserted, and each one of those present was there on his own, as if those were not chairs but so many tiny cells without the possibility of communication. So he continued

> l'Ammore è 'na palomma
> ca s'è fermata ccà

love is a dove that has settled here, and it was also clear enough that this rain was not about to stop, it was not about to stop at all. They knew it well, the Naples rain, which never falls or hardly ever, but when it falls it doesn't stop. And in the end from the windows of the Press Club there came that sticky dampness, that mellifluous smell of damp which, passing through the wallpaper and the carpets, reached people's shoes and feet, and there was no refuge, there was no refuge at all. The damp rose within until it reached your bones and slowly spread, and then those pains, like the pains of a creaking structure, and then you had to wonder: would it collapse from one moment to the next?

Because in fact from that third day of rain public transport had experienced very notable difficulties, and many lines had been closed, and many journeys cancelled on some of the routes that served the poorest districts, and maybe in terms of quantity that wasn't a terrible blow, because in fact there were few people in the streets, there were few of them now, but at seven or eight in the morning and at five in the afternoon there was always that stream of unskilled workers from the provinces, their hair stiff with dust and their combs in their belts and their fake leather bags holding their belongings climbing aboard public transport and cheerfully heading home again. Using the excuse of the bus going over a bump, every now and again they bumped into the cleaning women, but the cleaning women were aware of their little game, and no longer left their backsides exposed or very much in evidence, and instead they stood with those same backsides pressed against the cold metal walls of the big vehicle, and they were even able to escape the odd pinched buttock, and not that much harm was done, the important thing was that it didn't assume pathological intensity or manic fixation. Ultimately a hand on your backside, vulgar though it might be, is always an act of homage, a gesture of esteem. And after all there were as one might say notable difficulties with bus connections.

The buses passed in silence through big puddles, spraying muddy liquid up either side. This was particularly apparent on the Riviera di Chiaia, outside number 10, the location of the little Café Susan, run by Salvatore Picozzi, who had ten years before gone to live in London and returned two years later with the pure and melancholy Susan, she with the pale blue eyes and strawberry-blonde hair and totally in love with him because the first few times they had been together in the cold boarding-house room he had set to work with such enthusiasm that the poor English girl had had more fluid spurted between her legs during those nights than ever happened before save in her most unbridled nocturnal fantasies. Much time had passed since then, since those famous nights, a great deal of time to tell the truth, and you know what happens, a wife is always a wife, and you can't spend the whole day fucking her this way and that. In fact love is a great thing in what we might call the initial phase, but otherwise you have to adapt, and after all by day there are lots of things to be done, you can't just spend hour after hour every night pumping juice between your wife's plump thighs. But one would also have to say: the sweet enchantment of the foreign wife of Salvatore Picozzi had carried on in the years to come, when he had returned to Naples, in his district of La Torretta, because in fact all his friends and all his relatives and all his acquaintances always put on a big homecoming party for him because of that foreign wife of his and effectively expressed a marvelling respect for this thing that had happened in smoggy London, finding a young woman with pale blue eyes and strawberry-blonde hair. In reality, in his depths of his heart, Salvatore Picozzi had always felt a vague kind of self-important pride because of the marvelling respect that the others felt for his English wife, and he had convinced himself over time that his situation bestowed on him a certain pleasing prestige, and he had begun to look at his wife in a different way from other women. Because the other women were only and simply pretty Neapolitan girls and there were lots of those, really lots of them, with their tight jeans and the make-up on their eyes, but in fact there wasn't a single English wife in the district apart from his. His was youthful and delicate from the tips of her hair to her thin waist, she had fine, sweet northern features and gentle eyes that were sometimes cold but certainly unusual in the city of Naples, and it was only from the waist down that his English wife changed personality, from the line of her waist in fact there swelled truly majestic hips and big full thighs and firm calves. And all that hair, all that hair between her legs. Every now and again he remembered those first nights with her in the boarding house and how delighted he was to look between her legs because of that full red hair, and it was almost a mystery, almost, a surprise, an unexpected discovery. When he was indoors, in the warmth of Pub 24, rinsing the cups in lukewarm water, he thought again of that curly red mass of hers, and with a tender smile he found himself hardening. Those nights had been unforgettable, yes, truly, unforgettable for him and for her. Pure, melancholy Susan had writhed between the sheets like a crazed cat, and her convulsive thrusts and thrashing had continued over time, and in that unknown tongue of hers which he struggled to understand, she had said certain words she had said certain mysterious things to him, and he had never summoned the courage to ask her what they were. Not least because, once he had asked, she had told him candidly and with a serious expression that he must be mistaken, perhaps he had mistaken her for somebody else. Watching her reply like that, Salvatore Picozzi had thought at first that all women are whores, and the second thing he had thought was that perhaps he really was mistaken, perhaps another woman had said those lustful things to him in the English language. But as far as he could remember, he had been with no other women, apart from a couple of prostitutes in Soho and a young waitress from the same part of the city, who certainly hadn't said those things, and if they had they had done so in a profoundly different tone of voice. And in fact, that night, the general meaning of Susan's words had become suddenly and immediately clear, there was no mistaking it, but the problem had remained, because in a general sense he didn't want to understand, in fact he understood perfectly well, not the words in detail one by one, to understand precisely the terms used by that that woman who would subsequently become his wife and who subsequently knew other nights of unbridled lust with him, but because more than ever that night she came out with strange words said in that strange way. Sometimes, in fact, he had taken the greatest trouble in every conceivable way to wrest from her another night like that one, but he had never managed to do so, however hard he tried. That thought about her words had lingered in his mind, and in fact he too had tried to say a number of things, in the course of the unbridled embraces they had enjoyed subsequent to their time in London, but he had not been successful, no, he had not been successful. In fact, while speaking he had experienced a sensation of embarrassment, if not of actual unease, and indeed his wife had later delicately referred to his fragmentary outbursts. Also giving him to understand, quite clearly, because perhaps there was no need to insist, that perhaps his outbursts had the effect opposite to that intended. In short, Salvatore Picozzi wanted to say on that occasion but you – !, and he didn't say it, he kept it to himself. And there was that thought which now divided him from Susan. Because otherwise they had always lived a life of loving companionship. And Café Susan had been a warm and tender edifice that they had built together. For some time their life had proceeded in that way, with Salvatore Picozzi behind the bar and strawberry-blonde Susan with the pale blue eyes behind another smaller counter on the right as you came in, by the till and the little packets of sweets and chewing gum. Now there was that complicit tenderness between them. Sometimes they smiled at one another from a distance. In short, there was a secret understanding between them. He had developed something of a belly, in fact a considerable belly, not least because she had really learned to cook, and pure and melancholy Susan had assumed the habit of drinking a good glass of whisky after dinner, and sometimes two, or three, and then they went to bed under the covers and with that whisky inside them they made love without great acrobatics, but they did it really well, with that thing that went on and on, and in short it only occurred to him much later that she had come and in fact she had come more than once and sometimes in short they repeated those crazy nights.

Then by day they both stood inside Café Susan, she at the till and also answering the telephone, he at the espresso machine preparing the trays with the things for the little boys who were wandering about the place. Once when there had been a traffic jam that had lasted for hours and hours, he had had a brilliant idea and had started making coffee at very great speed, and immediately employed five of six of the little boys who had gone about among the cars selling coffee at twice the normal price. He had sold a truly indescribable quantity. Because in fact people would buy anything when they found themselves stuck in the car because of the traffic, and couldn't go forwards or backwards. He had also thought about selling newspapers, the day after the day with the coffee, but then in the end he couldn't reach an agreement with the newsagent. In fact the newsagent couldn't begin to understand his brilliant idea, he even objected that the traffic wasn't constantly stuck every day, which meant that this new initiative remained entirely hypothetical. You're best off on your own in the end. So the days passed like that, and since it had started raining for Salvatore Picozzi and his English wife Susan this had not been a big problem, because they had gone on peacefully making coffee as always. It only remained to be said that the number of customers had diminished remarkably during those days, but otherwise it really seemed that life was passing in exactly the same way as ever. In short, everything would be fine for some time to come, everything was fine, everything was agreed, had it not been for the holes in the road which during those days of uninterrupted rain had spread considerably until they became veritable trenches. And that had been the beginning of the problem with the buses passing no more than four metres away, and when the buses passed and took the hole outside from a particular angle, well, there was nothing to be done: from beneath the vehicle's enormous wheel, the rear wheel on the right, there came a spray of muddy liquid which reached the pavement and not only reached the pavement but also hit part of the tiny window and the front door of the bar which was tiny anyway and therefore vulnerable to the stench of that brown liquid which consisted of dust mixed with water. In fact Salvatore Picozzi took a great deal of trouble asking the people from the Municipality to intervene as soon as possible, because he certainly couldn't go on like that, and Susan looked at him with that steady gaze of hers while he phoned furiously and between her teeth she muttered some English words of disdain for the Italians, and he wasn't happy with that at all, but then again he wasn't happy about anything at all, and he couldn't help accepting that his wife really had every reason in the world to be disdainful towards the Italians, objectively speaking: towards the Neapolitans, because not all Italians are like that, some are even worse. And in short during those days the chance event of the puddles had become a resolutely endemic fact, a constitutional fact one might even have said. That had contributed considerably to the poisoning of his last three days, not so much on the grounds of economic disadvantage because of the constantly diminishing number of customers, not so much because of that as because of the fact that, fuck!, it's impossible to get a minute's peace around here! He had been given occasion to realise: in this city there was no chance of getting a minute's peace at all. Just when it seemed that everything should be proceeding smoothly and peacefully, something unpleasant inevitably came along to disrupt the deep-rooted order of those days and the life that was dragging itself along without any particular animosity but pleasantly, certainly pleasantly. Because in life it is plain that you can't have everything, and when you have a young English wife who's good in bed and good in the bar, when you have a little bar that lets you live peacefully and lets you buy your wife a handbag from time to time, when you have the wondering admiration of your neighbours and your acquaintances, and in short, when you have all that what else do you want? Or don't you want to spend your life breaking your back like the guy in Bar Renato, who thinks about nothing at all but the money that's coming in and coming in, and if it doesn't come in he really falls ill, physically, and his face turns pale. And in short what the fuck do you want out of life?, a sudden madness?, a split-second lack of reason?, a foul and hidden desire?, come on, tell me, what the fuck do you want? Had it not been for the puddles, these days right now would have passed calmly, but unfortunately those puddles were there, and then there were those bloody buses speeding up right outside the café and spraying a brown liquid at the doorway of the bar and spattering the whole floor and on a few occasions even hitting the calves of the customers, and this was a matter of the utmost gravity, certainly, he realised that. People would stop coming to Susan's for coffee the day they realised that coffee at Susan's risked ruining a pair of trousers with the muddy puddle-water. And in the end where did it say that he suddenly had to suffer because of this fucking Municipality that couldn't be bothered to maintain the streets in a decent way? As soon as the workmen arrived he'd give them a piece of his mind. Of course, that's what he would do. Even though he was perfectly aware, it was quite obvious, that the workmen did not bear any responsibility. They were just doing what they had been told to do. In short, do you know what the truth is?, the truth is that everything here is a mess, a complete mess, and when you want to pick a fight with an authority you can never find him, never really identify him, because it appears that everyone here is at ease with his conscience, everyone has done his own duty beyond a doubt, and in the end what is there left for you to do, beat your head against the wall?, come on, forget it, please, forget it.

Salvatore Picozzi was now behind the bar by the espresso machine, looking out of the window, into the sky, and all he could see against the light were those thin threads of rain coming down and coming down, and sometimes in fact he wanted to shut up shop, oh yes, shut up the whole thing and go home, but he said to himself that you can't do that, it's not possible. People are used to finding Café Susan open all the time during its regular opening hours. What would people think if they turned up for a coffee and found nothing but a nice closed shutter? These are unproductive things from a commercial point of view. In short, he stood behind the bar now checking those threads of rain, following the pattern against the lights of the lamps on the other side of the street, on the lights of some of the windows on the opposite pavement. And yet it was clear that the traffic had now thinned out, and there were really very few cars around, and there were few people in the street, and yet they passed at a nimble pace, wrapped in hoods and various raincoats, with black umbrellas. The women often carried gaudy multicoloured umbrellas, a splash of colour in all that greyness. The girls walked with a light, skipping step, with little squeals, and pauses, and jumps. Older women proceeded with that slow, methodical tread they had, steady on their feet, they had lost the lightness of the girls, yes, they had lost it some time ago.

And that was the third day of rain, 25 October, and no one had yet understood the matter of the voices hurled at the city from the arrow-slits of the Maschio Angioino. Nor was anything known about the dolls. There was only, for the moment, that vague memory of the memory of Sunday 5 August, and a vague foreboding, the curious hypothesis that would probably, with this rain coming down and coming down, change the very prospect of life. Some extraordinary event was bound to occur, somewhere in the city of Naples.

Margherita Esposito sadly reflected that this evening her son Luigi would not be coming home. He wouldn't be coming back, and this time wasn't like the other times it had happened before, when maybe her son had been out all night for some encounter he had with a member of the opposite sex or perhaps he was out of Naples somewhere, no, this time it was all different, because an awareness had descended of the fact that he wouldn't come home, he never would again. From that night onwards, and for all the nights to come, he would sleep with the girl he had married, and in short that piece of her heart had gone forever. The house was poorer and sadder now. Something was missing. Margherita Esposito wandered around the house, and checked, and checked, and without a doubt something was missing, she was aware of the absence, that was it, she was aware of it, and it was certainly the absence of that young son of hers who had gone. That night she didn't feel sad, perhaps, but diminished, yes, diminished. Someone had taken away a part of her, and she found herself poorer, perhaps also more alone, thinking about it, but Margherita Esposito wanted to avoid thinking about it. So she went on wandering around the house with a duster in her hand. She ran it over the furniture, and over the mirrors, and over the windows, and to tell the truth there wasn't much to dust, but what was left in that harsh moment but to wander and wander around the house?, what was left? The rain hit the windows of her house in Posillipo with a tender and sweetly melancholy sound. In some respects it was a caress, that rain that fell to obscure people's feelings, that vague hubbub in the distance. Were the walls about to fall down?, would the house disappear?, what? The duster went around in a circle on the dining table, following the trace of a mark until deep into the night, a mark that won't fade, a firm solid dry thought which this rain is dissolving and removing. Perhaps she might half-close her eyes, feel in her eyelids the start of tears that refuse to fall, were it not for that duster going round and round in a circle on the dinner table, and for the life that goes on. Because to tell the truth they can pull your arm off, they can mutilate your legs, and pull both your eyes from their bloody sockets, and they can burn the skin on your hands, and everything, but this life will go on as before. Your only option is to breathe hard, and stay calm, keep a strong grip on yourself and breathe right now in the silence of the night, and listen to your breath as it rises and falls, and the sound of the rain. Adding it up, it was the third day that this rain had been falling as it was falling, the third day in a row. If anyone wanted to believe in omens, let them. She could read her coffee grounds for portents, and find a meaning in the arrangement of a pack of cards. That ace of spades, why that ace of spades?

*

And beneath that rain that was coming down slowly, he quietly advanced, closed away inside his car. On the windscreen the wiper drew ellipses, greyish filaments and quivering lights. When he turned into Corso Vittorio Emanuele he knew that this time he would do it. He knew it in a flash of illumination, like a full headlight shone into the street. Then he changed gears and pulled over to the pavement on the right, so that anyone behind could easily overtake him. He felt in his chest that strange sensation like an unbidden emotion, and how would it end up he wondered, but there wasn't much time now for those belated questions, because along the street in the headlights those unusual figures were emerging with their red-painted lips and their gaudy dresses. Their high heels, their densely drawn eyebrows, and their black and blonde and fire-red hair. It seemed to him that they had emerged as an interdiction, a prohibition. You can't do this, you can't do this, and yet it needed to be done, then, once and for all. Certainly with the requisite caution, but undoubtedly it needed to be done. In brief snatches Alfonso Amitrano ran through his own personal history, and this was the third day of rain in the city of Naples and through the windows he could make out the pattern, and it was possible to conjecture that from one moment to the next an unusual and in some respects a cruel event was bound inevitably to happen. Certainly an event out of the ordinary. And had the disaster on Via Tasso and Via Aniello Falcone had been an omen of what was to come?

*

That precise awareness had reached the devotees of the Holy Face. Now, inside the Sanctuary, everything was being put back into his hands, in such a way as to provide for what was just, for what was truth, and in fact truth is always very difficult to attain, and when you have attained it someone always appears to give another, different version, and this new version undoubtedly also contains an element of truth. Sometimes you find yourself thinking that the truth has a thousand faces and is in every place and in every person. Within the Sanctuary the image of the Holy Face descended to take fear from the palm of your hand. There was this trust, and the meditative silence, those prayers, those people murmuring on their knees. Outside the Sanctuary they were selling the image of the Face in the form of a car sticker, and everyone had his own. In fact, some people had more than one, on the four corners of the rear window of the car there were four stickers neatly arranged, and then there was the reassuring image of him with his blond beard and his blue eyes. Once outside of the Sanctuary, let us put it this way, one felt at ease, with one's mind more agile. He had delegated; yes, he had delegated. Now there's nothing more to think about, nothing more to worry about. The Face had been appropriately filled with hidden fears, hopes and thoughts. And even if that unusual rain continued outside, even the rain was more bearable now. The dark foreboding remained, certainly it remained, but with no reason now to worry. Or perhaps there was, but anyway.

*

It was on that third day of rain, 25 October, that the five-lira coins began to play music, and one might have thought at first that it was the result of a collective hallucination, of autosuggestion. But that would have been an impression that did not correspond to the truth, because in fact all possible and imaginable acoustic measurements had been made, and we know very well that if it is true that a brain can be rendered suggestible, the same does not hold for a recording device, and in fact every time a recording device was called upon to confirm the song that had just been heard, the reproduction corresponded to the reality in every single particular, and if the verification of such an unusual phenomenon was initially entrusted to devices which were not especially sophisticated, we must also say that highly sophisticated equipment was used to address the problem, and each time a check was made the result was the same as the one before. Because in the end it was clear even to the most recalcitrant that this was not a matter of suggestion, nor of collective hallucination, but of actual, genuine music. Well, it would also be appropriate to point out that Sara Cipriani was nothing more than a ten-year-old child with long blonde hair whose mother washed it constantly because she wanted to make a good impression on her friends, and on her fellow tenants in the building at 324 Via Posillipo. Sara Cipriani was four foot seven inches tall and without overwhelmingly brilliant results attended the fifth-year class of the Alessandro Manzoni primary school. In short, she was a likeable little girl, sad by temperament but still always cheerful, already with a melancholy hint of adolescence in her eyes. She spent her days going to school in the morning, from half past eight until one o'clock, and then she came home for lunch, and before eating she brought down her cocker spaniel puppy and then she sat down at the table with her parents and her brother. Her mother was always saying to her don't do this, don't do this, and in fact she paid attention except that sometimes she was distracted by a fleeting thought, and then maybe she made a mistake, and if she made a mistake her mother was immediately ready with that shrill voice and no gentleness at all. Then she bit her lip in silence, and accepted those reproaches, and lowered her head, and her father didn't say anything to her, but then her father never said anything to anybody in that house, he just gave you those long looks sometimes that burrowed inside you, more than once she had thought that her father's eyes were beautiful and gentle and deep and they reached you like a caress, like a tender smile. In short every day they came together around the table at about two in the afternoon, and her mother always had lots of things to say, especially to her husband, but her husband said not a word in reply, he listened, certainly, he listened carefully to every word and every syllable, but then in the end he said nothing at all, if there was a problem in the end he gave a nod of agreement to the solution already put forward by his wife and in short those family meetings at two in the afternoon passed wearily and were always the same and several times Sara Cipriani had reflected that perhaps everyone in that house lived for themselves, yes, for themselves, and there was no cheerful confusion or lively conversations, but the silence that fell was disheartening. Immediately after lunch her father left, he got up from the table and said well see you later and put on his raincoat in the hallway and at the very last moment just as he was about to leave she arrived in silence, she got up on tiptoe and kissed him on the cheek, he stroked her long hair with his big hand and then opened the door and closed it behind him, and then he was gone, he was gone for another day, and she was about to stop for a moment and think about it, when her mother's voice came from the kitchen saying that she had to give her a hand, didn't she?, but she was always pretending to forget, she had no desire to help her mother, in the kitchen after lunch, even though she understood very well, of course, she understood: it was something that had to be done, and in the end she cleared up carefully slowly bringing the dishes to the kitchen and putting everything else in the drawers and took the bundled tablecloth and shook it in the air from the open window. When it was all over, she said do you still need me?, no I don't need you, her mother replied, and then on tiptoe Sara Cipriani crossed the corridor of the flat and went and threw herself on the bed in her room, with her arms crossed behind her head and her feet crossed and her eyes wide open staring at the ceiling and after a while she heard vaguely through the corridor and the half-open door that her mother was on the phone to her friends. Then, so as not to hear the women's chatter which was always the same and the same again, turned on her portable radio in the shape of a Coca-Cola bottle and lay there listening to music, and with music the afternoon certainly became more bearable, dream images crowded into her eye, from the window overlooking Via Posillipo came voices and the sounds of cars and buses stopping right under the building, and generally speaking that's how things were. Until one day her mother said wailing and red-eyed you've got to stop being annoying!, and let me show you what's going to happen to that radio!, and she picked up the radio in the shape of a Coca-Cola bottle, went to the window, looked out and hurled it into the street. She heard that faint sound of a frail thing being smashed. Sara Cipriani wanted to say, and wanted to do, but instead she stayed on the bed with that lump somewhere in her throat taking her breath away and after a while she felt two big tears running down her cheeks, silent and unseemly, and from the open door to the corridor came the words of her mother saying over and over how tired she was of having a daughter like that?, and what did she think?, with that other one who is never at home and never says a word even if you pay him!, can you believe the two of them?, was she their servant? Sara Cipriani got out of bed and tiptoed to the window, and down in the street she saw her radio in the shape of a Coca-Cola bottle and there was nothing to be done now and silently she went back to bed and crossed her arms behind her head to take a deep breath and crossed her feet and lay still crying inside and showing nothing. She wouldn't say a word, no. She wouldn't say a single word. Her mother could break all her things if she liked, she would never say a single word. What did she expect?, that she would cry?, that she would go and ask for forgiveness?, that she would sweet-talk her into letting her have the things that were actually hers? Oh no. She could take everything away every single thing and throw everything down into the street and do whatever she wanted and she could even hit her in the end, but she wouldn't say anything, not a word, her strong, hard silence would become an impregnable raised barrier. And she lay still reflecting that now the afternoon was really longer and more interminable, without music, without the songs of her radio in the shape of a Coca-Cola bottle. She put her hands in her pockets and tightened her shoulders, and then she got up on one elbow and threw all her coins on to the bed. 225 lire: one hundred-lira coin, two fifties, two tens, one five. The five-lire coin was absolutely tiny and teeny and light in the palm of her hand and for some reason she brought it to her ear, perhaps coins were like shells, and you could hear the sea if you listened very carefully in silence. It wasn't the sea that came, not the faraway swish of an echo of the sea but music, music that she could clearly make out, yes, she could make it out, and she immediately recognised the song, which was the song about Lily, the girl who takes drugs and dies and they should have stopped her in time and treated her and instead none of that had happened and Lily was gone, gone forever, and a playful smile appeared on her lips, and her eyes opened wide at the discovery. The five-lire coin repeated in her ear the song about Lily and all the other songs she liked, and in the end she had only to think about a song and immediately the coin repeated it to her and now she had all her personal music, her truly personal music, and no one could take it away from her no, really no one. To check she took the coin away from her ear and as she had predicted the coin stopped playing, and then she brought it back and again she was listening to a few songs and then she gripped it in her fist and put it back in her pocket being careful to put the other coins in her pocket on the other side. Because the other coins didn't do a thing, they were just ordinary normal coins, one hundred, two fifties, two tens. And in short she put that five-lire coin in her right pocket and touched the velvet of her trousers, and that same day, at that same moment, in all of the houses in all of the city ten-year-old girls found that their coins were playing music and there was an incredible crowd of parents who wanted to know and wanted to hear, but in fact when they picked up the coins and brought them to their ears they couldn't hear anything at all, only little girls heard the music. In fact, as we have said, at first this phenomenon was considered rather suspicious, and people thought it was something to do with auto-suggestion, with a collective auditory hallucination, and then proofs and counter-proofs were necessary, but in the end when all the tape recorders supplied the same identical response it was clear even to the most sceptical and recalcitrant that it had nothing to do with suggestion and everything to do with music, which the tapes faithfully reproduced, and which no one could then deny with a shrug or by saying but anyway you know what little girls are like, always daydreaming, because in fact all the little girls all over the city weren't actually dreaming at all, and nor would they dream in the future. They just brought the five-lire coins to their ears and out came music and songs. Every afternoon throughout that whole period all the little girls all over the city were rich in that music that came out ceaselessly, and at school from desk to desk they started exchanging coins and one girl already had the idea of buying them up, of collecting as many coins as possible, but after a while it was clear that buying up coins was completely pointless, you could have ten or a hundred but the one that played music was the one and one only, and in short even the most recalcitrant saw very clearly that there was nothing to be done but give them to girls who didn't have any. Violent disputes broke out among the mothers about the quality of the music, because some of them were convinced that their daughters' coins played much better music than the coins of the other little girls, so those stories circulated around the city about the previous evening with every detail about the music that had been played and the songs, and everyone emphasised the beauty of a tune, the cadence of a phrase, and furious debates raged among the mothers about the superiority of this or that kind of music and in some cases these arguments actually became physical, women were seen scratching each other's faces, pulling each other's hair out and even rolling around in their sagging nylon stockings and fake eyelashes and girdles and bras and big black lace knickers and in short it was quite a confused time altogether. In the streets of La Torretta and Ferrovia street vendors appeared, dealing in counterfeit five-lire coins because they had immediately come up with the idea of exploiting the situation, but however hard the operators of these makeshift clandestine mints might have tried, it was clear to even the most spendthrift buyers that there was really nothing to buy, because without exception those coins did not play music and they never would. In the meantime the local academic authority of the City of Naples along with the Office of Public Education decided to launch a series of promotional demonstrations encouraging the dissemination of musical culture among the school population, and at the Polytechnic Artistic Circle a series of highly learned meetings was held in the course of which long discourses were delivered concerning the advisability of stepping up and defining pedagogical musical interventions in schools, and this seemed to be a necessity that could be put off no longer even for those people who were least responsive to music, so much so that the school year was interrupted from one day to the next and in effect resumed from the beginning only seven days later, when the programmes concerning what would in future constitute the musical education of the population were prepared in detail. We should add that alongside public education during those days a series of private institutions of musical instruction were also set up at very short notice, and unfortunately after a certain amount of time had passed it had to be admitted that the music teaching at private institutions was both more profound and more practical than the teaching carried out in the state schools, and on the other hand you know how it is, certain tasks cannot be accomplished from one day to the next, but in short a great step forward had been taken, and some private institutions were already planning to restore the Scholae Cantorum of the seventeenth century, along with the inevitable castration of boys and young men interested in following the courses, when fortunately a memo was circulated by the Ministry of Public Musical Education in which the practice of castration was condemned once and for all as a barbaric, medieval practice, most severely prohibited save in exceptional instances which had to be authorised on a case-by-case basis by the relevant authorities, but on the civic level it would have to be added straightaway that the harmful phenomenon of castration remained limited to a very few regrettable episodes, and in short the bulk of the population, in spite of the obvious advantages that could derive from such a practice, remained calm and peaceful, without giving rise to a resurgence of seventeenth-century practice. More than anything they were in fact impassioned about the great variety of singerly events which from that point onwards were authorised and put into effect at increasingly frequent intervals, and of course you will all remember the famous Day of Song, at least in its first, monumental version, when the stadium of San Paolo di Fuorigrotta was filled by a hundred thousand children truly belonging to every social class, all dressed in white, delivering a huge and admirable interpretation of 'Funiculì, Funiculà' in the presence of the Head of State himself, who attended with all the members of the Council of Ministers in the central circle of the pitch, at the precise spot where every game kicks off, and on that occasion Naples was literally invaded by the special envoys of the national and international press, and a British broadcasting channel somehow managed to acquire exclusive rights to the show, which it then sold at an increased cost to other broadcasting channels within the western bloc. In short, that Day of Song, in its first and monumental version at least, was a truly unforgettable day. Key rings and banners had been manufactured in the shape of treble clefs and the City Council had authorised the installation of two thousand kiosks for the impromptu sale of souvenirs, and there was a packed press conference by the Mayor, a poor, flabby, perennially sweaty man who stressed in a suspicious voice that, through this tangible trial of strength, Naples had regained its pre-eminence in the field of the world's music, a pre-eminence that had for too long been the prerogative of barbarian populations worthy of branding with the mark of the most reprehensible musical superficiality, and in short this was truly a great day for the city which lingered indelibly in everyone's memories, and at the end of the performance of 'Funiculì, Funiculà' the same Head of State, assisted by the Ministry of Musical Heritage, pinned to Sara Cipriani's white pinafore a gold medal with a treble clef on one side and on the other the words Naples – First Day of Song. Had it not been for the rain that was still coming down, it would have been a perfect day, and instead because of the rain an awkward question remained and something like a sense of unease that even music could not totally erase. In short, everyone understood that beyond the essential fact of these musical coins there was still something that was inexpressible yet concrete, extremely concrete, and it was precisely in that clash of lucky presentiments and embarrassed uncertainty that the third day of rain, 25 October, came to an end at last, and when people later recalled it what remained was mostly confusion, something like an accentuated disarticulation of the city, which felt it had lost its peaceful tranquillity and which still did not feel it inhabited this tremendous event that was yet to come, oh quite certainly, it was yet to come, everyone was willing to swear, and it would alter all perspectives on everything. Along these damp hidden streets of the city nothing survived but waiting, and a treacherous disconcerting provisionality descended to weigh heavily upon everyone's thoughts and nothing survived, nothing apart from that sad and desperate thought that probably everything was about to change. Ships might drift and women in love would bleed from their nails and the geraniums on our grey balconies and terraces would shed leaves of their own accord. How, in the end, do we tell the story of that distorted anxiety that climbs, and pants, and groans, and that voice that sails and flies across the asphalt: on his hands now it descended to press on the provisionality of an inconclusive gloomy and unbreakable presentiment which still drags glowing decorations down into the mud of anxiety. It goes on now, it goes on drawing assents to shame, to uncertain fear.

And when, at the end of the third day of rain, it was 25 October, Carlo Andreoli found himself clutching that inert mass, night had fallen many hours ago to enclose him in the circle of waiting, his eyes were red and swollen now, they pressed against his eyelids. He was clad in fear, he felt cold and hard beneath the fabric of his shirt, and many hours had passed now, many hours, and the whole day had passed now, and he was left with the fatigue that had assailed his knees, that had forced its way into his nerves and tendons. Sadly now he went back into his house and stayed there listening to the sound of the door closing behind his quivering back, and stood smelling the silence of the dark house, and from outside the rain drew questions on the troubled breathing of the city, and the flat was sweet and empty and silent.

Carlo Andreoli felt as lonely as a limping dog. He felt his feet in the corridor and he felt his heavy swathed clumsy body falling on the bedcover, and in the fear of night he lay there with his eyes open reflecting and nothing appeared before his eyes, nothing apart from little black dots, and however much he traced things back and forced his breathing and set his gaze alight, he could grasp nothing, nothing at all, and the anxiety and the fear and everything, but he was weary now, let Naples crumble, oh yes, crumble. And he closed his eyes.

THE FOURTH DAY

The fourth day of rain was 26 October, that is to say the following day, and this day announced itself with a pale and changing dawn, as if the morning lights were pressing on the horizon, and still nothing appeared but luminescent greys and the rain came down softly as it had done in the course of the night. He sat up in the middle of the bed to reflect: somewhere there must be a key to understanding. Running his hand over his face he saw from his window rivulets of rain carrying mud and detritus and drenched papers and stones, little twigs of shattered trees, debris came down from the hill of Posillipo towards the grey mirror of the sea in the distance. He heard the sound of the child from below, sitting down on a high wall, under cover from the rain and outside the range of adult hands, beginning his grotesque repetitive chant and insistently hysterical laughter, and how many times had he heard it and sometimes stood watching him: the child made himself comfortable on the wall and waited for people to pass by, and if a girl passed by he immediately said with that blank and stinging voice of his what lovely legs you have, miss, what lovely legs you have, and then he started laughing, laughing, his laughter stretched out in time and for long minutes, accompanying the girl into the distance and far away and even when the girl couldn't see him any more and had disappeared and was gone the echo of that incredible cheerful laughter still remained dragging on in time and for long minutes, hee hee hee hee hee hee hee hee hee hee hee hee hee hee!, and then an old man passed by with glasses and a hat, with the serious step of Dignified Old Age and he from his wall said what a lovely hat you have, what a lovely hat, and then off he went laughing with his shrill and stinging laugh, with those high and penetrating notes, hee hee hee hee, hee hee hee hee hee hee hee hee!, and noticing the sound of the child from below Carlo Andreoli reflected that it was getting late, that he had slept enough and too long that night, and now with this new day of course he had to move if possible. Even if indubitably he also had to reflect on where to move to?, because in fact the problem was still there, full and harsh in front of him in its entirety, and none of it had been eroded, not even its thin crust: his poor journalist's brain had found itself impotent and ridiculous when faced with this great round ball of problems from the previous days, and this day too and everything indicated that the thing would go on like that, in this way, with no chance of recovery. Had it not been for the fact that it was nearly a new day, he would have thought forget it, because in the end it wasn't etched in stone anywhere, but in fact the real truth is that you can't, no, you can't, and even if the beautiful key to understanding existed somewhere, complete with its various accessories, perhaps everything began at a precise spot. That was it, start from one spot and disentangle everything, detail after detail, and in the end it would come out, oh yes, it would come skipping out, that ridiculous and insignificant truth, and then perhaps someone would say to themselves but how stupid not to think of it before!, and in the end there was the determination to start again, that much is certain, but still there was the going about the house, and looking at himself in the bathroom mirror before shaving. Looking at himself like that he thought of the time when he was sent to Via Cavalleggeri d'Aosta because a woman had died and no one knew quite how, and he remembered it very clearly that time, because as he passed through the hall he noticed clearly and immediately that if there was a place to die that place was definitely the one beneath his feet right now, and it was a strange and cruelly unusual sensation to feel beneath the soles of his shoes that if there was a place that was fit for death, well, that place was beneath his feet right now and who knows why. But in any case he climbed the flight of stairs and on the first floor he went into the flat, that time, and there wasn't much to see, not much, with those two wretched rooms and that acrid smell everywhere, an inexpressible stench, and then he also saw the woman at the foot of the bed and he took a photograph and everything, but he didn't remember it because of that wretched corpse, definitely not, it was more because of the unsettling memory of the two windows in the bedroom overlooking the street, and from the street he had already noticed that those windows were all covered with reddish dust, of course, and that dust had become layered starting from the four corners of each window, and in the end it happens everywhere, in the district of Fuorigrotta and in Bagnoli, but this time no one had resisted the reddish dust, that was it, no one had opened the windows and no one had gone with a cloth in their hand or with a duster to remove this dust, no one had done it, and the reddish dust had accumulated day by day on the two panes of the two windows, from the corners of each window it had risen to the centre, and covered the whole of the surfaces until no light had been able to enter the house. That same day, as he drove back towards Coroglio, reaching the second hairpin he found himself pausing on the way down, and beyond the street, towards the sea, there was a park and patches of green and a few trees, and a few couples dotted about the place fooling around, and that was the spot, he almost recognised it, where he felt that sweet thing within him, tender and benign. Because one day one year long ago his father had said you see?, it was at that precise spot in Coroglio, one far-off day many years ago, that Grandpa Nicola first fooled around with Grandma, and in that phrase that he had uttered there had been a son's quiver, and also a faint smile, and a thought, and a profound pondering look, that time he had looked at the precise spot and had seen nothing, nothing at all, but now that he had stopped on his own something seemed to have survived, something had escaped, perhaps but how far away and how indecipherable. And so it was that Carlo Andreoli stopped looking at himself and said, fine, let's shave then. From the white cabinet with the mirrors gently and slowly he took his razor and brush and the little tub of shaving cream, and turning on the left tap he let the water run until the water was hot, and then he put in the plug and for a moment he stood watching that scalding water steaming and steaming, and he ran a finger along the blue porcelain and an opaque trace remained for a moment and then vanished. There was this clear fact, and this doubt, and also a decision to be taken if possible. A faded light fell through the frosted glass of the bathroom, if you listened carefully you could hear the muted sound of the rain coming down for that fourth day in fine threads as it had fallen for the three previous days, and who knows for how much longer, how much longer. In fact let's say that the situation in the city had worsened considerably, not so much because of extraordinary events, because in fact nothing at all extraordinary had happened, the usual emergency phone calls and requests for assistance to the fire brigade, a piece of cornicing had fallen off here, there a sinkhole had opened up, and the cellars below, some streets had been rendered entirely impassable by the rain and the blocked sewers that had ceased to flow, an ancient buttress set up to maintain a shaky building on Via Santa Teresa degli Scalzi had also shown signs of danger and unsteadiness, a containing wall had collapsed on top of the parked cars, and nothing in short that was extraordinary, nothing at all. In many factories in San Giovanni a Teduccio they hadn't even started work because of the water and the public transport that now worked barely at all and services were constantly cancelled, and in fact really sometimes you don't know how to get by, and because of a flash flood even the underground train had stopped that morning, and a team of engineers was trying to get some kind of understanding, seepage of water on this scale was far from normal, all they needed was for water to come down on the underground train every time it rained, some hope, in this fucking city, but from a wall that suddenly opened up there came that endlessly gushing flood of water, there were cobblestones on the rails, bouncing across the wooden sleepers and on the two polished iron strips. The glass of the bathroom window brought him the voice from below, Franceeescaaa, and for a moment Carlo Andreoli paused to hear if Francesca would answer, but Francesca didn't answer and the person who had called thought it best not to press the issue, because perhaps it was entirely pointless, perhaps Francesca had gone down somewhere with her girlfriends, twelve-year-old girls always have lots of things to tell their friends, and they have these delicate budding breasts, in their eyes the uneasy melancholy of the woman who is already on the way, and quick oblique hidden glances, and because of that faint light that was coming in he decided to turn on the light and there with that light perhaps it would be better: when he went downstairs to get the car and Francesca was out and about, Francesca gave him a secret look with that serious adolescent expression, and he looked at her too, and after a while there came the nudges from her friends, stifled laughter, hidden jokes, and he couldn't, of course, there was nothing he could do, and he reached the car, he locked himself inside, set off, went away, truly away, remaining dozy and without the words even to wonder what you can do in such situations, and he would have liked to, definitely, certainly he would have liked to, but what can a man of thirty-five say to a little girl of twelve, what could he say?, in what tone of voice?, with which words?, and now maybe with that rain coming down and coming down they would shut themselves away in a bar somewhere smoking cigarettes and listening to music and would have around them the right little boys their own age, maybe a bit older, and that encounter would erect a further division, another, different separation, and then nothing more, nothing at all, and with the electric light on everything went very well, yes, all very well, apart perhaps from the reflections in the mirror, and in the end you can never have everything in life, you make do with what you manage to grab as best you can. In the end, Carlo Andreoli picked up the shaving brush in his right hand and considered its bristles, and when he pressed them they bent obligingly, and he stood there thinking, and then he set the brush back down on the porcelain and decided that it would be better to soften his beard manually, and in fact rubbing his face with his fingers he felt skin that was distinctly below par, along with the previous day's beard which woke at the contact there was the skin that was a little weary and chapped and flaking in places. Doubtless at that very moment Francesca was hidden away somewhere with her twelve-year-old anxieties, and otherwise what was to be said, my friends, what was to be said, had he not had his own justified anxieties at that age?, and what was it that troubled him back then?, a sordid little envy?, a mean disgusting envy and nothing more?, everyone has the right to his portion of years, and what do you want?, to repeat the experience?, have a bigger portion than anyone else?, and why? In fact he was left with nothing at that moment but the sad awareness, and a tepid smile in the right-hand corner of his mouth, and Carlo Andreoli went on admiring that smile and then he curled his lips to reveal his moustache, moustaches are always so ineffectual in the morning, and in the brief moment in which he remembered Maria he saw again the house in Castel Volturno in the sunset that can't be seen because the sun has gone and night with its white lights has not yet come, and there was that greyness all the way to the sea, and the sound of dogs barking, and that flat strip of beach, and I will never go back there, I will never go back, I can't spend my summers in a place like that, he had said, and with his fingers he had shaken his black hair, and that black expression of his had returned to look at him from within, and he went away, oh yes, she was speaking with that uncertain voice of hers, and meanwhile she was moving irremediably away, she was going in silence and moving away, and she had that strong vivid life within her, Maria, her non-negotiable rights as a young woman, and perhaps she was only in love in a manner of speaking, perhaps she wanted to force herself to experience what she was thinking, but life is always different, different irremediably, and it never coincides, never, and like two thieves they had entered the house with a fist through the closed window and made love in the cold damp silence, voices of caretakers and sounds of cars reached them from the darkness, every now and again, from the unpaved streets and alleyways, and that impressive silence of salty damp air, and around the house there was no sound but the words spoken by the two of them, and then irregular breathless panting, and then that sweet arabesque ahhhh! that went on and on and modulated with the contortions of the fall, and she followed him, she followed him to the end as a tender woman in love to give him warmth, and perhaps there was also that fear of the caretakers who might come, but none of that would happen in all likelihood because in truth there no one guards summer houses in winter, and in his half-lidded iris there was still a long strip of sand with the reflections of the last of the light, and dark shapes falling obliquely, and the still silence, and the noise of dogs in the distance, and the shrill sound of birds, and there was still that face of hers laid bare defenceless as if to say this is the settling of scores, is that it? Curling his lips, Carlo Andreoli stroked his moustache on the right and the left with the index finger and thumb of each hand, but the hairs returned to their previous position of their own accord, moustaches are always so strange in the morning. He took the tub of shaving cream and dabbed a finger into it, then spread it over his face trying to cover every single spot, and then he put his finger in the steaming water and spread it over his face, because the cream dissolves more easily with a bit of water, and it had dissolved in fact and then he gave himself a brief delicate massage with the whole palm of his hand, and beneath his palm he felt that skin of his, and now he renewed his acquaintance with his own face, even though in truth he continued to avoid meeting his own eye, afraid as ever that the mirror would return to him an image that did not really correspond to the way he thought his face must be at that moment, and in fact more than once he had wondered if the image he had of his own face corresponded to the image that other people had of it.

Because of the rain that was still coming down, along the facades of the buildings greenish rivulets had formed, and in places the plaster had come away and in others it showed stains of uncontrollable greenish damp, and there was that non-resistance, in the end, which ineluctably accompanied the falling rain, almost exhausted all capacity to react, as if the will had degraded into mossy patches without consistency, and along the walls the damp drew the outlines of each stone in mildew. The question remained of whether the stones would resist, with all that water coming down and coming down on that fourth day exactly as it had fallen for the previous three days, and in short it did not seem that the city intended to react, restricting itself solely and simply to absorbing the water for as long as it could, but the problem in fact is precisely that: to what extent can water be absorbed?, what in reality is the tipping point? At any rate it was as if this problem were still indistinct and confused and certainly a long way off, because resignation had turned into indifference, and in life you get used to everything. If the city too had to change its sunny destiny into a new and different rain-filled destiny, well, even that change would have been accepted, because in life you inevitably accept everything, and in the end in life life is endured, and then if the days to come had been grey and rainy it would have caused neither traumas nor open wounds, and in all likelihood even in that new dimension advantages would have been discovered, points in favour, but one would also have to say that without a doubt, along with such considerations, at a first level of reading others were confusedly formulated, and beneath the damp that reached the bones and wrinkled the eyelids, a confused and ungraspable current stirred. A vague and sinister apprehension that shook and shook and turned in a circle and darted suddenly to the surface before returning back down to the bottom where it continued its constant irregular movement, and still in people's breasts that obscure apocalyptic question swelled, a presentiment of misfortune, an event that would alter the perspective on life. In those uncertain days of waiting there was nothing left to do but wearily survive and delay, delay everything, because in fact it is a very cruel operation taking away the prospect of a future however unlikely, what are we to do with these men and these women, and this whole city?, without a future however unlikely how do you send your children to school, get married, do what needs to be done to move house or apply for a government grant? Those thoughts were his very thoughts, because the fact of knowing the story of the doll and the story of the voices that had appeared on the first day did not in fact in any way shift the terms of the problem, any more than it determined different sensations, or different theories, the provisional state of that vague waiting was a transparent crystal flower, not a series of scattered fragments, in fact there was that beautiful concrete crystal flower on one side and on the other the uncoordinated disconnected thoughts that could not lead back to an underlying thought, no, they could not do that. And there was now no option but to take into account the greyish reality that was attacking the foundations of the buildings and digging rivulets into the asphalt and eroding the tufa of Posillipo.

That aquatic reality had in the meantime assumed aspects of particular and immediate dramatic force especially in the district of Afragola that centres around Corso Vittorio Emanuele, because the water had undermined the uncertain foundations of a series of houses that rose precisely above the underground tunnels, and Christ!, was this city built on a void?, and the big fire engines had breathlessly arrived in the rain once more, and there had been a clearance and a dozen families were now accommodated in the elementary school on Via Marconi, but of course no one could imagine that this would be a solution to the problem, certainly not, because in fact in terms of accommodation it really left much to be desired, and blankets of coarse wool had been brought and urgent supplies of milk had been brought at least for the youngest children, and then all supplies had ceased because it had been noticed that the goods were constantly leaving the council warehouse but never actually reaching the school, someone somewhere was skimming it off, and initially in those times of extreme confusion it was impossible to identify the jackals so there was no option but to suspend all supplies. A delegation from the Council Welfare Office visited the council as soon as possible and then proceeded to identify the households and list the homeless and even that simple accounting task was not an easy one, in that the children were literally running in all directions and you could never work out if that one there with the black curls had been counted already or not, and then you had to take into account the children who had been temporarily removed, and then some women didn't want to provide information, talk to my husband, I don't know anything, and all in all it was necessary to trace each husband one by one and overcome those suspicions, and only just towards the end did it become reasonably clear that there were eleven households in all, a total of a hundred and fifty people, because you also need to consider that in many family units there was not only the head of the family the wife and the children, no, there were also dismal toothless irascible aunts, slobbering old women with dirty blouses constantly complaining that this is a sign from God, that this is a sign from God, and in fact they would come to understand over the days to come, they would understand, lots of people were scratching their balls and saying *sciò sciò ciucciué* to ward off evil and touching wood, and the old folks replied go on, touch wood, touch wood, because touching wood does no good anyway, this is a sign from God for your wicked behaviour, what do you expect?, it means nothing to us, absolutely nothing, because we haven't long to live anyway, but what are you going to do?, eh?, what are you going to do?, but in fact even though they said they didn't have much time left, it was clear to everyone that they were firmly attached to life and trying desperately to cling on to it, and this was not just a reaction like many others, and when they had finished counting everybody, a hundred and five in all, in the cramped council offices the decision was made to involve the Prefecture of the City of Naples in the case. Inside the school a series of folding beds had been set up with those heavy woollen blankets, and the children were really happy about what was happening, because in fact the school was the school they went to every day, they were very comfortable there, and they knew every single desk, the teacher's table, the blackboard with the coloured chalks, the maps on the walls, the big illustrations with the letters of the alphabet, and in the end they really didn't feel they were in a cold and inhospitable place, in fact they were entirely at ease there, and it was only much later that they realised that with all those fathers and mothers around they couldn't enjoy themselves as they usually did. And the mothers decided that each of them would stay close to their own children to avoid confusion. When the news of Afragola reached Naples along with other more or less similar news, some people said responsibly: we will come to harm here if this rain continues. In fact many people turned their faces towards the sky, almost as if to check, but there was only that grey, high up, with that rain coming down and coming down, interminable as an animal's agony.

After massaging the skin of his face with his palm one last time, Carlo Andreoli ran a little water over his hand and dried it, and once it was dried with that same hand which was still his right hand he picked up his shaving brush and soaked it in the hot steaming water in the basin, and he held it there for a moment and squeezed out a little of the water but not all of it, so that the brush was still sufficiently damp and wet. As ever it was an operation, in fact a series of operations, that needed to be performed well and with great attention, because the brush must not be dry but not too wet either because otherwise it wouldn't foam up as it should. Then he checked that everything was in the right place, and set the brush back down on the porcelain, and with his left hand he picked up the tub of shaving cream, and with his right hand he took off the cover which he placed upside down, and looked inside the tub and saw that white, shapeless magma. It was then that Carlo Andreoli thought of escaping, of course, of escaping, and in fact it was a strange thought this thought that was running through his mind, because escaping meant resolving nothing and even more so it meant, in practical terms, giving up and surrendering, if you put it like that I'm not doing it, and in fact he was not returning to his habits, he was not returning at all, and on that greyish morning drawn with threads of water he could have got into the car and crossed the strange city and reached the motorway and then gone far away, to another place where things were different, where the rules of life were concrete and precise. Without that sad softness, without that sentimental weariness and lazy intelligence sighing after lunatic ideas. Of course, he would stay behind the wheel for hours and hours, and he would see the landscape changing and changing again, and little rocky villages at the top of the hill, and lonely towers, and truck lights in the night, and service stations, their attendants washed out with exhaustion, and inside in the darkness at the end of the night he would stop somewhere to have a steaming hot coffee, and he would move his neck to the right and left to stretch the sinews, and he would look around at the advertising posters and the special two-for-one offers, and he would buy a pack of American cigarettes, and he would sit and wait in the car with that hot cigarette in his hand while the tank filled with petrol, and in the end they would run a sponge over the windscreen and then dry it with a chamois leather, and he would turn the key in the ignition again, and as it made contact all the lights would come on and the engine would draw out that engine noise and he would slip into first, gently passing the yellow lights of the streetlamps, the red lights of the waiting cars, and there, all alone in the night, he would find himself, with that need to go on and go on that would not leave him be. In the end, he would certainly arrive in another city, a different and unknown city, and what difference do you think this one or that one would make? If you leave your own city, your own place, everything else is the same, always the same where you are, isn't it, everything is to do with severing the umbilical cord, once it's severed then everything is the same for ever, and also you see, and you realise, you never belong to anything, not even to the sum total of roads and reasons that seem like your city, in fact you never belong, and even when you do belong there's always that hidden zone of the mind that refuses and curls up in a ball. He would get out of the car into a large and tree-lined square, he would hear behind him the sound of the door closing and with the lit cigarette in his hand he would walk around a bit here and there, looking at the people in the streets and the girls and the windows and the trams rattling along the rails, and after a while he would go into a bar and have a steaming coffee and would ask: excuse me, which city is this? And in fact it would be a strange thought because he knew very well how attached he was to these stones, and that desolate, grey life of the sea in October, oh of course he knew very well, however unusual this thought that ran along furrows and convolutions and appeared in his half-open eye observing the confused white magma of the shaving cream in the tub that he was holding in his left hand. Then Carlo Andreoli looked at his right hand holding the brush and dipped it in, and with a rotating motion of his wrist he went on turning round and round, until a milky foam was born and grew visibly in the tub, until it gave off the smell of almonds that he always noticed every morning when performing this operation, and he turned the brush around again a little to be sure that the foam was strong and dense. A bit of foam spilled down from the tub, fell silently into the steaming water in the basin and then dissolved gradually until it disappeared.

The news of the clearance in Afragola had created an undifferentiated growth of panic and apprehension in the operational centres of the city, oh there's nothing else to be done with this rain but to follow the rain, and wait for warning signs, catastrophic signs of collapses and chasms, and in truth it was not only the news of Afragola, but that alarm certainly represented a link in the very long chain of dramatic omens and similar events that had appeared more or less everywhere, Sant'Antimo, San Giorgio a Cremano, Pozzuoli, Casoria. Not knowing where to turn, the fire chief, if only out of a qualm of conscience, had also called the meteorological office at Capodichino airport, and in truth no clarification had come from that office, in the sense that the metallic voice at the other end of the line had listed a series of cyclones and anticyclones which in other words provided the sad confirmation that it would go on raining as it had in the last few days in the days to come, and it was reasonably thought that if they who were the meteorological technicians said so then there was no point looking at the sky every five minutes, because it would go on as it had gone on, there was little to be done, very little, just waiting, and lighting cigarettes one after the other, and promptly transmitting any messages that came in, and if the fact of having to suffer caused a silent fury that would have liked to take concrete form perhaps in cursing and swearing if nothing else, it would also have to be said that the explosion was prevented or halted, halted completely, by that vague but concrete apprehension that in fact those alarms were merely the ominous signs of what would really happen, of that extraordinary event that no one knew but which everyone now expected from one moment to the next, because they did not know at least another full day would pass in a not particularly distressing way, they knew only about the grievous event on Via Tasso, where a whole family had been wiped out because of the bureaucracy of Social Housing, and the grievous event on Via Aniello Falcone, where the rain had undermined the road's supporting structures, and the road had collapsed taking with it the young and undiscussed life of Rosaria De Filippis and the strained and colourless life of Wanda Zampino. This was all they knew, and it wasn't much, and also, sad though the facts were, no extraordinary event had taken place, and in the end these facts still belonged to the realm of the possible, until that moment they belonged to the realm of atmospheric adversity, which for good or ill in some way in the end they would succeed in harnessing, Naples had experienced days even worse than the ones it was living through now, it would manage at any rate, oh of course, and it would get through this awful time, and in the summer that would later blossom these rainy days would be nothing but a disagreeable distant memory to be erased as soon as possible, let's put a lid on it, shall we? This awareness gave people confidence, in truth, even if that kind of confidence hour by hour did not seem enough, it was not enough at all. In fact, everyone was tracing within themselves the faded signs of fear, which redrew themselves, a little at a time, on the supply of news coming not only and not so much from the poorest areas of the city, as from the immediate periphery and the surrounding villages, and it was quite certainly as if a siege had its grip on Naples, and the circle seemed to be shrinking with each hour of rain, with every alarm signal, and the suffering and rage would certainly have exploded had it not been for the fact that they were still waiting, they were still waiting for an extraordinary event which would overturn and alter their perspective on life itself. In fact, listening to the old people's stories, this situation today was not serious enough to fill hearts with anguish, because they very clearly remembered that Naples had experienced even worse days than the ones they were living through now, and in the warmth of the pool halls they told stories of the famous Flood of Vergini, a deluge that swept away everything and entered people's houses and destroyed their ground floors and ruined shops and bars forever, and you couldn't walk in the streets except in rubber boots and walking on wooden boards, and that had been a very sad time, at least for those who lived in the district of Vergini, and they remembered very clearly, and that was a much more serious situation, oh boy, much much more serious. Today you can't understand these things, today everything's all neat and tidy, but in the old days it wasn't like that, oh no, and you really had to earn your living, and when that unstoppable sea of water came down, there was no point shouting or cursing, oh boy, your only option was to roll up your sleeves and get to it, and put your back into it, and try to salvage the unsalvageable, and stack up all the furniture in the house so that you didn't lose everything, and you had to upend the box springs and the mattresses. In fact, these stories by the old people, terrible though they were, seemed to some extent reassuring. Then, in the pool halls, you could also have a game of 10-card scopone, or a game of bocce, with that fluorescent light falling on the green baize and the scoreboard placed at the side, and all that remained in the breaks between one shot and the other was an involuntary dart of the eyes towards the window in the door to check the opaque image of rain still coming down and coming down. It hammered against the windows. The people who came in came running in saying fuck! the rain!, and they were breathless and dripping, and the people who left stopped in the doorway to look and didn't leave at all, they stood there with their hands in their pockets instinctively waiting for it to stop, and then when it was clear that it wasn't going to stop, then they turned up the collars of their jackets and fled beyond the windows and they could no longer be seen clearly, and every time it looked like a farewell, as if they were making a lonely escape never to return. Because with that rain coming down and coming down drawing circles on the asphalt, everyone felt more alone, and they all surprised themselves by lowering their heads, and a hundred conscious thoughts ran through their minds, and everyone even said that it seems as if we should be drawing some sort of conclusion, but what is it?, the day of judgement? But in fact for now there was nothing but those vertical threads of water plummeting towards the earth and the sea. And then, with his soaped brush, Carlo Andreoli soaped his face, taking care to spread first a uniform film everywhere and then returning to each point with a rotating motion of his wrist which covered in order his left cheek, his chin, his right cheek, and then beneath his jaws almost to the neck. With the firm and regular movement of the brush, the foam grew again and now became soft and agreeable, yes, agreeable, and this white part was now homogeneously softened, and in fact he knew very well: it is chiefly the passage of the brush over the skin that decides the good or bad outcome of a shave. And when he had finished he made only a few upward adjustments towards his cheekbones and over the right-hand side, and at last he set the brush back down on the porcelain and for a moment he paused at the mirror to check. The mirror returned to him the twisted question that kept coming back and coming back, that endless question that he tried where possible to repress, but which always rose up once more to cloud him over with a malevolent sense of awkwardness, of inexpressible unease. It threw his thoughts into chaos. And the thoughts left each of their own accord like bits of gravel in the wind and nothing managed to reassemble in the air but a pattern of provisionality, and you can't live in provisionality, it has been scientifically demonstrated, and swirling in the void is the consequence both ineluctable and painful, even though he knew: the brain was working on its own behalf. Of course, it was working, and it would draw out the solution at any moment. And when that happened, the dead on Via Tasso and Via Aniello Falcone would be nothing but the most ordinary accidental deaths as happens every time it rains and when following the rain a collapse occurs or a sudden subsidence of the road surface, and he waited for that moment in a state of uncertainty, and he wasn't sure in fact that it would come, not sure at all. In fact, looking carefully around, his precarious condition was the very sensation of awkward uncertainty that the city enwrapped in its greyish cloak, woven of greyish filaments, coming down the grey hill towards a grey sea. The desolate uniformity of tones, and the silence dragging itself along the line of the horizon, and in the street a few bundled passers-by hurrying under the rain, and a drinking fountain in Mergellina with its jet of water, and the cracks in the plaster on the Palazzo Reale, and the painted words on the statue of Dante Alighieri, and the plastic bin bags piled up on the street corners, and the unpaved stones of the Galleria della Vittoria, and this was what remained in the end, only this, and perhaps one day things would be different, perhaps one day the city would flourish once more, but for now the only option was to pull the covers over your head and wail gently. Illness had swept away the tinsel and the brilliant decoration, and had extinguished the cries in the street, and the geraniums on the balconies had turned yellow, and the cheerful fiction/pretence of collective action had now transformed itself into a harsh statement of loneliness. And this remained, of the priceless city, only this, and the shadow of a faded past and the rhetoric that claimed it was poetry, and nothing, and nothing, and which other city would one day live?, which city?, the city of alleyways and transvestites and smuggled cigarettes?, or the city of the New Polyclinic, the Bypass, Secondigliano 167, what would one day become of the life that climbs today among the tufa quarries of Fontanelle and the green trees of Floridiana?, and what are we going to do with this sorrowful city?, do we want to separate it for example?, that's it: do we want to erect a playful granite wall all around it with gorse and mimosa trees and then divide it from the rest of the people? In a city like that lovers could hold each other's hands and ask the City Council if they could remain young forever and ever, the women would have unfamiliar girlish voices, such a city would lack the anguish that now mortifies and lays siege to our hearts, the dark premonition that with this rain coming down and coming down will come the unforeseen, the extraordinary event that will upset the seeds in their furrows and burn the plane trees of Vomero, and raise the asphalt of the streets, undermine the stones of Petraio, turn back the sea. In such a city there would not be this sad waiting that now spreads to the sinews of our hands, pressing pressing and stopping every single thing, that restless waiting of consciousness that runs through a whole life checking the signs along the path, and in the end you are left with nothing, nothing but an exhausted expression and a tremulous voice, accursed city!, I will hang your women with their legs in the air on the highest battlement of Castel Sant'Elmo and leave their heads dangling in the void, I will mutilate the legs and eyes of your children and in the streets I will peer into thousands of prams containing those deformed little monsters, I will cut the fingers from the hands of your men and throw mercury into their veins, I will throw cow shit into the halls of the Palazzo Reale, and the rooms of the National Museum, and cow shit into Villa Pignatelli and the Certosa di San Martino, and bring donkeys to piss in Via dei Mille and in the Galleria Vanvitelli and the yellow brew will fill the streets of Vomero and Chiaia, I will scatter pigs' guts inside the shops and bars and in all the offices in all the city, and this you will become, my city of sorrows, nothing but a heap of rotting malodorous offal, and your stench will mingle with the stench of the diesel that I shall pour on the sea to cover it, this you shall be and nothing else, a stinking yellow rotten puddle, with miasmas of encroaching decomposition, your big abandoned whore's body will be putrefaction, squalid unstoppable shameful death. With these sobs and jolting spasms, Carlo Andreoli raised his razor and paused to consider the edge of the blade. And the heavy plastic handle. And the precise point where the sideburn ended and the soap foam began. And then at that point, with a precise gesture, he brought the razor down, and the blade descended to his cheek, and from below the blade the hairs of his beard could be heard crackling before the cut, and it slid, yes, for now it slid well. Five or six passes of the razor, some long and defining, others short and corrective, he finished shaving the whole of his left cheek with the growth, and suddenly washing the blade in the hot water he then began in the opposite direction, because however much he might have seemed to have cut, in reality without going against the growth you are left with an unsatisfactory amount of stubble. This time he was careful to ensure that the passage of the blade was lighter, and while the razor rose again accompanied by his right hand, with the other Carlo Andreoli held the skin of his face taut, on his cheek level with his cheekbone, and then sideways almost level with his ear. The soap fell of course into the hot steaming water with the black dots of the cut beard, and a kind of oily patina formed and floated on the water, and the light reflected in the mirror and he was forced to crane his neck to see, and from the blue maiolica tiles of the bathroom the reflections multiplied in the confusion of meanings, in the inconclusive chaotic superimpositions of a life that had certainly been chaotic and inconclusive. He found himself reflecting that on the first day an agonised mournful roar had hung over the city and from the towers of Maschio Angioino it had unearthed fear, awoken the hidden stones of the hidden city, the urban mystery of a city stratified into vague magmas of contemporaneity, and there had been an exploratory mission within the castle and in the end a doll with black hair had been discovered and identified as the endless source of the terrible sorrowful voices, and even this had not been the extraordinary event but only the prologue, the prologue and nothing more, because in fact he knew very well and all the other inhabitants of the city knew very well: this had been merely the start of the transformation. A succession of slow and degrading modifications would break down the city's present life. Of course somewhere in the shadow of the church a priest would set the chalice back down and come and sit on the first chair in the first row, and He would come down from the cross and from the altar, and He would sit down sharing that sweet weariness, the composed silence, and nothing but the two of them sitting there would survive in the church, and without words, completely without words, but that was clear, wasn't it?, it was extremely clear that He shared his thoughts, and that elegance of the hands. Grass would grow in the cracks in the marble, spiders would weave cobwebs, on the fresco at the back mildew would advance slowly and inexorably, and flowers would sprout from the base of the marble columns, and flowers, and weeds, and a very great deal of time would pass in that ineluctable silent way, days would follow days, and outside more and more faintly those voices of the life that went on and went on would keep coming, because that life itself goes on, and only after long years of mute understanding, at the doorway, in the sudden slant of light, the figure of a little boy in short trousers would appear, and only then would they get up, to leave, leave once and for all, time for a change of shift. And he also found himself reflecting: now all that was left was to wait for another day, a whole day whose every tremor he probably knew in advance, every tiny event that would occur, and you can't do that, no, it's impossible to live already knowing, it's impossible, and how would he spend those inexpressible twenty-four hours?, reading the practice and discipline of yoga?, castles in Spain?, information and mystification?, how would Carlo Andreoli spend that day of his that he already knew? In this question there now appeared the awareness of a sudden theft. Yes, life had robbed him of a whole day, a whole day of 24 hours punctuated by minutes and seconds, it had robbed him of a sunset and a night and that inexplicable darkness that always comes down with the evening and had robbed him of an exuberant awakening, with the light of the day coming in, flourishing once more, he had simply been cheated of a day that no one would ever give him back, no one ever. But in the end he would remember, of course, and at the right moment he would draw his winning card: ah no!, another moment, I have the right to one more day, and he would produce the documentation, certainly, he would arrange his cards neatly on the table, and that way he would provide his certification, with various stamps and seals: another whole day still awaited him, and certainly thinking about it now a day seems like nothing, less than nothing, but think a little about whether they might give you back this extra day in the end, try and think: there, let's say that you are in bed and at some point the communication arrives: dear sir, with reference to the warnings we have sent in the current year, we regret to inform you that your game is definitively terminated with immediate effect. What would happen? What would happen is that you would collect yourself sitting in the middle of the bed and say to yourself with a smug smile, ah, no!, dear sirs, no!, as documents in my possession clearly reveal, I was cheated of a whole day, twenty-four hours precisely, which I was assured would be returned to me at the end, and it is not as if I want to bring the game to an end, not that, I could certainly not put up any resistance, I know that very well, just as I know very well that it would be pointless for me to come out with considerations concerning my young age, etcetera etcetera, except, my dear sirs, I now demand respect for the rules of the game, just as I have respected them, and they would have no choice but to carefully check the cards, consult one another in mysterious confabulations, and once the authenticity of the claim and the validity of the documents produced had been ascertained, they would concede, however reluctantly: ah yes, sir, you are right, wait another day, twenty-four hours precisely, and at that point albeit provisionally the matter will be closed, they would leave the house in silence closing the door behind them, and you lying in your bed would go on reflecting, with a smile of satisfaction, and one day, oh yes, a whole day to live!, sweet eternal wealth would have appeared to him, inestimable, playful wealth. In that definitive, radiant day of his Carlo Andreoli would go the chalet on the gulf with books and newspapers under his arm, a pack of American cigarettes, the box of safety matches, he would make himself comfortable in a wicker chair and on the chair opposite he would stretch out his legs and remember, yes, he would run through that brief and tender season, the flowers, and the poetry, the smells of girls, and his beloved work, and the city that stretched before him, the flickering lights of the night, the memory of his father, the sweet sweet skin of Mavie, the books under his arm when he went to school, the football games in the middle of the street, and how strange it is to have in your hands a fistful of flies and perhaps not even that, and how sweet that life was, in that new and different dimension the perspective really would be overturned, and certainly many of the things he had struggled for in the past he would not struggle for now, oh no, and furthermore he regretted nothing, nothing at all. He would spend that crucial day of his like this until sunset. He would see the line of the horizon blurring, and purple-grey shadows would come down, and with the cold air of the first evening he would come back inside the house, and in the library he would confront the countless backs of books with the fingers of his right hand, and how much how much he still had, how much he had left to do, would never do and with a big book in his hands he would make himself comfortable in the armchair and read, yes, he would read for ages, every now and again raising his eyes to the vague familiar things, and the thoughts of the book would interweave with his own thoughts, this thought of his right now that was squandering his last few hours, and this playful love that would grow between his fingers, would spread and flourish with sap and tender white petals, in the conscious serenity of a smile he would say well, let's see what happens now, and from the window he would give one last look at the city spread out below. With a deep sentimental sigh, Carlo Andreoli checked that his left cheek appeared perfectly shaven. Strange how the skin comes out regenerated in the morning, fresh and uncontaminated, young as a young man's skin, and then, turning his head to the left, he took his razor to the edge of his right sideburn and repeated the operation with the greatest possible attention, because one of the fundamental errors is that of losing concentration, in fact you shave on one side with extreme care and diligent attention and then you don't even notice and you lose your concentration, you become distracted, you get caught up in your own thoughts, and on that other side you end up cutting or scratching yourself. No, my dear friend, you're not going to mess me around this time, here too my hand will be as light as a butterfly's wing. In fact he discovered that the razor was proceeding exactly as it was supposed to, and let us say that the shaving of the right cheek was a complete success, and by way of checking Carlo Andreoli ran two fingers over it once more and received confirmation, and in the end everything was for the best, that morning that was the fourth day of rain. That superficial sensation of well-being rising gradually would remain unchanged throughout the entire course of the day, certainly, and the day after, in all likelihood, because he could not really see how his graceful sense of balance could have been thrown out of kilter. Not least by virtue of the fact that he was aware of everything, and that compared to others he had the advantage of serene consciousness, and he alone had heard the roaring groan from the arrow-slits of the Maschio Angioino as a calm event already foretold, and the loud sorrowful thunder hurled against the city had dug no deep furrow in his heart, and he had waited for that inhuman cry as if of multitudes with his muscles tensed, and he had stood motionless noticing the anxiety of the city and the frantic agitation of wretched men. The voice from the street reached him again, Franceeescaaa, and the shrill laugh of the boy somewhere, hee hee hee hee hee hee hee hee!

In the bus shelter, Adriana Cuomo looked carefully at the clock. 8.20. The bus probably wouldn't come, and she was about to say right I'm going home, I'm going home now, and she repeated it to herself, but even inside she was aware of the fact that it was still her duty to go on waiting, better to turn up late than not to turn up at all, and in the end think about it: in life you always have some kind of duty to perform, imperatives on all sides, and lots of people saying you've got to do this, you've got to do that, in your place I would do it like so, if you really want my advice, no, thank you, I don't want anybody's advice, I can make my own mistakes if that's what it's all about, and in the end let's go on waiting, bah!, who cares anyway, however much I've got to do, however much I might enjoy myself at home perhaps it's better to go to work, and she also thought how strange it is: when you're a child you never want to go out really never, and when you go out you can't wait to come home, and perhaps you don't want to go to school one morning, and you dream of staying in bed, or going home with some excuse or other, you see, sir, I don't feel well, and instead you're big and grown-up and you weigh in the balance this house of yours and working at the office, then inside you opt for work, oh not work exactly, let's understand each other, but in the end the fact of going out, yes, of going out, closing the door behind you and going into the street and seeing the people and looking at the shop windows and dodging the traffic, and darting tender hidden glances when necessary, and perhaps work too, yes, perhaps the work is better too, because sometimes when you're at the office you actually see strange and amusing people, and handsome boys too, sometimes. Adriana Cuomo gave a sidelong look at that man with the grey coat who was standing with her in the bus shelter and she said he's waiting, of course, he's waiting, he doesn't look impatient at all, at that age you probably don't have anything to do, and when you do have something you have all the time in the world, old people are always extremely calm, calm and dignified, they don't run in the street, they don't raise their voices, perhaps day after day they are doing a dress rehearsal for death and they will be practised enough, and in the end it won't be a trauma, it will be a matter of emphasising a condition that is already in many respects familiar. The man with the grey coat stood stock-still with his feet together, with both hands in his pockets, and on his left arm he had hung his dripping black umbrella, and underneath he had a grey jacket, a white shirt, a patterned red tie, pomaded greyish-white hair, a very thin moustache like the kind people had a long time ago, from one generation to the next everything is so deeply different, even moustaches, and shoes, for example, the cut of people's trousers, and sometimes you should stop to reflect that these old things aren't ugly, they are just old, but how in a girl's day do you find a moment like that to reflect, a cheerful young girl has no time at all to form reflections like these, because in any case those days really fly by, and who expects you to stop and ponder?, and by the way, my friends, you've had your time now make room for the others, what do you think? A long look down the street returned with this image of the falling rain and nothing else, and Adriana Cuomo sighed heavily, and as she breathed her ample breasts swelled, what breasts, boys, what breasts, sometimes she did it on purpose, she stretched herself, she stretched her torso up from her hips and breathed heavily, and when she did that her breasts rose magnificently, really magnificently, one day a boy had told her, those are magnificent,

I have no other words, she had smiled, and in fact at first those great things in front of her were more of a nuisance than anything else, because to tell the truth they bounced around in all directions, but then we would have to say it had turned out over time: there was also a good side to the whole affair, in the sense that, unlike others, she certainly didn't go unobserved, and in fact she had sometimes turned them, as we have said, into an instrument, and then let us also say quite clearly and firmly: when you find yourself in bed making love, and you feel those men's hands, and you see the looks, there's a kind of legitimate satisfaction in it too, isn't there?, if men pester and pester to get at that thing between your legs and want to hear you say how big you are and how beautiful, constantly how big it is and how beautiful, you should let women have their pride too, shouldn't you?, or are men allowed everything and women nothing at all?, and in fact the first few times at least she went to bed she had tried to repeat the statuary poses that she had practised in front of the mirror, her arms in the air, to lift her breasts, for example, or her arms with her elbows tight to her hips to lift them even more, and in actual truth really the first time her tragic embarrassment had seized hold of her as an overwhelming feeling of panic, and all she could do was wrap the sheets around her shoulders and try in short to cover herself in every way, and turn on to her belly to hide, but in short it hadn't been possible, not possible at all, and in the end she had yielded to his glances and explorations, and then once and for all she had faced his questions, why are you being a fool?, what does it matter?, they're not ugly, they're a bit on the generous side, maybe, but they're far from ugly, you know how many girls would like to have ones like yours!, and then in all in all she had joked about it too, yes, and then she had realised, sometimes we become fixated on really silly things, and maybe we don't confront problems, and problems grow and spread, when then in the end it's enough for someone to say who cares, and it all goes, everything completely, or at least that's how it seems. Adriana Cuomo sighed heavily and from her handbag she took the piece of paper and when she felt her fingers identifying it among the various bits and bobs, the rolled-up banknotes, the small change, a tube of cocoa butter, her bus pass, her identity card, the mother-of-pearl button from her other coat, then she withdrew into a corner of the bus shelter and rested her hip against the strut and glanced at the rain that was coming down vertically and splashing against the asphalt, and she took out that piece of crumpled paper and turned it around in her hands for a moment. But she had already made her mind up anyway, she would read that exciting love letter one more time. In fact she knew very well there is no more pleasant sensation than reading a letter from someone who has lost their head over you and is writing nice words to you, and at first it's really something stormy and romantic, let's say you're fourteen or fifteen, and maybe you think that as life goes on it will stop being like that, and maybe it isn't like that any more, maybe it isn't like that for a long time, but then, when it does happen, immediately once again that romantic adolescent spark comes alive again, in short let's agree that it isn't exactly the same when you're twenty-four, not that, but there's always that sweet itch, it comes back straight away every time, who knows if it comes back when you're fifty?, and then again she spends her time turning and turning in her hands that little piece of paper, and she feels an itch in her fingers, and in the end it's a pleasant sensation, nothing to be said. Let's open it for a minute, see what it says. My sweetest love, well yes, his love, that would be me, last night after I phoned you with agony in my heart which I was feeling perhaps for the first time, and painful too, well, I'm not very sorry about that, because your refusal to meet up seemed absurd to me, no reason for it, and what do you care?, but now I want to tell you: it doesn't matter, Adriana, it doesn't matter at all, however many times you tell me no as many times I will return to the task, because you should know this: I love you with a strong, lasting, indestructible love, lucky you!, and you will be able to stay far away and go out with other people and refuse to see me for as long as you like, but in the end you will have to surrender: I will always hold out one day longer than you. Goodbye Adriana, Marco. And as she sighed she cast a glance along the street, to the bend, to see if by any chance that blessed bus had made its mind up to come, but there was really nothing to do, there was no sign of anything, and what about hitching?, but who would you hitch from?, because in fact thinking about it very carefully you realised that a car passed every now and again and nothing more, always at high speed, splashing water in all directions, and then what do you do?, if they don't stop what are you going to do, and in the end her look had returned nothing but that desolate grey whole, and how strange it is, she thought, every time the weather changes the mood of the people changes too, if the sun's out you wake up cheerful and sprightly, if it rains you're sad and disconsolate and you don't even want to get out of bed, but why?, do you believe all those stories about the influence of the stars on human life etcetera etcetera, where did you read that?, a book, once, a long time ago, yes, it talked about all those things, and the signs of the zodiac, she was Cancer, nasty sign Cancer, fickle, easily influenced, very dreamy, who knows if it was really so, in fact when you try to analyse it you can't, you're always forced to trust the judgement of others, oh but let's see: my sweetest love, he wrote, while the lawyer didn't write anything. There, now that she came to think about it, all that time, the lawyer hadn't written a thing, not even two lines just to be kind, every now and again however he gave her a little present, a silk scarf, a handbag, a pair of boots. He was a solid type, the lawyer was. Sometimes with his back to a client he came over to the typewriter and wanted her to touch him, or else he rubbed herself against her back, saying with a wink: make sure you do a good job, miss, because this is an important thing, and the first few times it was amusing, but then in the end you weary of it, men are disconcertingly vulgar, really, with their sniggering and their innuendos. Oh at first she had been amused as well, you see, sir, I have a big thing here in my hands, sir, let's see if we can't take care of it as quickly as possible, it's urgent, and in short it had been funny, and they had gone on calling each other miss and sir in bed as well, or rather to be precise on the sofa in the waiting room, because they had never been in a real bed with sheets and everything, he always said he had no time, on the one hand, and besides his wife kept a constant eye on him, and then at the office it was much easier, and even if his wife phoned at the precise moment when he entered her, there was no problem, certainly darling, fine darling, see you later darling, and his wife had once even said I think you're making fun of me when I ring you up, you really are daft, he had said, and for her birthday he had sent her a big bunch of red roses. When will this impossible rain stop? Perhaps it wasn't really what you would call a big romance, not that, but in the end it was better than nothing, certainly better than silly boys like Marco: my sweetest love: yeah, his sweetest love, and in some ways she felt tenderness towards him, yes, with those glasses always slipping down to the tip of his nose and him constantly pushing them back up again, and once he had sent her three orchids in a transparent cellophane box, she had been happy that time, really, how strange it is, sometimes a thought like that can straighten out a twisted day for you, bah, and now she went on turning that letter around in her hands, its writing slightly feminine to tell the truth, who knows, the lawyer had told her some really disconcerting stories about men, and then she had checked in person: if she stroked him from behind he rose up at the front, and perhaps that doesn't mean anything, perhaps not, but it's certainly a strange thing for a man, isn't it?, he had said it's like that for everyone, there's nothing anomalous about it, nothing irregular, and in some respects it had struck her as a very strange caress, a caress like that, and above all it made her laugh, yes, sometimes she found herself unexpectedly helpless with laughter, but at any rate that lawyer of hers knew what he was up to, he was the lawyer for the Traders Association, with all those consultations, all those questions, and he also did labour cases, where he was always halfway between the two parties in the case. And in the end he worked to ensure that in the courtroom they always so to speak reached a settlement, yes, a settlement, and once he had even explained to her: it's very simple, you have to tell the worker that we risk losing the case, and then say to the defendant: I'm going to save you a lot of money, call it a day, and in the end everyone was happy and he said to his client you see?, I've won you a hefty sum, haven't I?, and to the other side he said I've saved you a packet eh?, a real packet, and in short it worked very well, with all that paperwork of his, and above all with the telephone, he spent whole days on the telephone, and when is it going to stop raining?, is there not a chance of that blessed bus coming, I'm going to hitch, that's what I'm going to do, I'm going to hitch. The man with the grey coat was standing in exactly the same position, hands in his pockets and umbrella hanging from his left arm. God knows where he was going. In the end it probably wasn't a big romance, this one, but who cares, for now she was getting a fantastic salary, and presents. To tell the truth, after the first few frantic times it wasn't as if the lawyer jumped on her every day, hour after hour, in fact the amorous contact had been getting rarer and rarer for some time lately, and mostly he amused himself with innuendos, silly little jokes, sudden shoulder-rubs, or else he would have some ludicrous idea, once he had said miss will you do me the honour of not wearing knickers during working hours, and she had been in on the joke for a whole day slipping off her knickers and crumpling them up in her handbag, and in short for the past few days everything had been very peaceful and calm, it was probably about to come to an end, but it would be a problem in any case, and less because of the lawyer than because of the work, she had to work somewhere, didn't she?, if she wanted to stay on her own and independent, unless, that was it, unless she started to think about having Marco as a husband who would work for her, and then she would be in the house, and he would shower her with kindness, yes, shower her with kindness, and when she went to hospital to have the first in a long series of children he would turn up with big bunches of flowers and boxes of chocolates, that's usually how you have babies, isn't it?, he was a strange character, Marco, really a strange likeable kind of boy, and pleasant and understanding and nice to be with, and he was delicate with her in a way that no other men ever were, that was true, except that he never gave her that jolt. However much he tried, however well disposed she was, in fact he never managed to give her that jolt inside, never a spark, a fury, an enthusiasm, in short anything to shake her up, and Adriana Cuomo knew very well: if a man can't give you that jolt on his own there's nothing to be done, it's not as if you can help him, but in any case the idea of Marco as a husband she put in the corner, who knows, in life you never know, life's such a mess, sometimes you think you can never do a particular thing and then you find yourself doing it, or vice versa, and now I'm going home, now I'm going home, but then she remembered that no, that day she really couldn't, there was a meeting at the office, and the people from Colorac would be coming, that lawyer of hers had been appointed liquidator, certainly in all that mess he would manage to get some decent money out of it, perhaps she might get an extra little present, who knows, certainly it wasn't a cheerful situation exactly with all those people out of work who didn't know where to turn now and were still in charge of the factory, like that, so they didn't give in straight away, but in fact what's someone without a cent going to do with a factory?, a factory seems so important that you say now let's occupy it and see if we can't reach some kind of agreement, but then in the end you realise that they're going to get along just fine without a factory, you're the one who can't live without your salary, and then maybe things drag on for months and months and in the end a new buyer turns up who's nothing but a straw man for the old owner, and then the state gives him some money, and he puts it in his pocket and then maybe a year later we're exactly where we started, the lawyer had even explained it to her once, the grant mechanism, to hear him speak setting up a factory is the easiest thing in the world, to hear him speak you don't even need any money, because the state gives it to you and then you have to give it back in thirty years' time, but it's not as if you're held to that in person, no, it's society, so if society goes bankrupt, for example, nothing is given back to anybody, and in the end she was left there in the bus shelter with her hip resting against the iron strut and that note from Marco in her hands, and in her boots the damp that was coming from outside. Then she curled up her toes a little trying to move as much as possible, but this rain that was falling now was bound to go on falling as it had fallen for the previous few days, certainly, there was no sign to suggest the opposite, was it possible that those days of hers would go on passing in exactly the same way?, for how much longer could that playful seesawing between Marco and the lawyer keep on going? In fact, thinking about it carefully, there had already been some warning signs, oh yes, she had clearly identified them, just as she had identified and catalogued as far as possible that restlessness that she now found in her hands, that anxiety about a change that was about to occur, and what exactly would change?, her life as a woman?, her relationship with the lawyer?, Marco's flattering attentions?, would she leave Naples?, what exactly was hard to say, yes, very difficult, not least because in some respects there was that solid certainty: her young life as a young woman would change, and she would see other, different events, and it would never again be like this one that she found herself living once more, without a doubt somewhere along the line it was preparing a jolt for her, that was it: a jolt, she would be overwhelmed by it, and she would live the days to come with an intensity that she could now no longer remember, or perhaps she had a vague recollection of something, like her teenage years, for example, when it took nothing, really nothing at all, and she had that marvellous ability to surprise herself and to wonder and discover things, and every day was an adventure, and at night she lay in the dark with her eyes open thinking incoherent thoughts and dreaming up diaphanous schemes, and that future never came, life is always different from what you think, and then perhaps you almost need to stop thinking, how do they put it?, go with the flow. She stood there thinking that if she had waited for the bus for all that time, now she could just carry on, it would come in the end, wouldn't it?, and anyway here I am now, why would I go home?, for what reason? The rain came down with methodical regularity making vertical splashes on the asphalt, and then the water collected at the side of the kerb, it channelled itself down the street, and there were manholes that should have absorbed it, but now they were absorbing absolutely nothing at all. In troubled rivulets the water dragged along runnels of pebbles, bits of paper, corks, sweet wrappers, there were those tiny sweet things that the water dragged behind it. Up above the greyish streaks alternated and merged, a variety of shades of grey drawn on grey.

And Carlo Andreoli said well, let's move on to the most difficult phase, and with his left hand he pinched his cheek stretching the skin from the bottom up in such a way that it was taut over his chin, and from the left side he shaved with his razor, and he felt the blade passing, and with three or four strokes everything was fine and then he repeated the operation on the right-hand side, except that on the right-hand side he had always had greater difficulty, but it went well that morning, yes, it went well. In fact, when he had finished passing the razor over the middle of his chin, he checked that this shave really was a work of art, impeccable, a proper shave lasts you until well into the night, and of course it puts you in a good mood, it is a kind of good omen for the day, and on a day like that one having a good omen was something extremely positive, who knows what would happen, on a day like that, above all who knows what decision he would decide to take. Because it was undeniable that a decision needed to be taken by him personally, since he was the one who knew about those strange things, and about the sorrowful roar that had engulfed the city, and the mystery of the dolls with the black hair and the dress with white yellow green flowers, and in the end after a moment he had a sense that the very life of the city was in his hands right now, certainly, in his hands, insofar as he was vaguely aware that he might be able to do something in everyone's interest, if he moved in the right direction he would take an important step with considerable consequences for everyone, and it was a responsibility, an insurmountable responsibility that he was now weighing up. And he also reflected that in fact it wasn't really like that at all, in fact whatever step he took would define nothing whatsoever, he knew only and simply about a certain number of inconclusive things that would in any case have been impossible to connect with real events, with concrete facts, and even if he had told everyone about what little he knew, no general meaning could be taken from it, and no precise clue: they would be fairy tales, ravings, of course, and why not?, wouldn't he have thought the same if they had come from somewhere else?, if they hadn't been something that he had touched with his own hands?, what confusion, lads, what confusion, we should just wash our hands of it all, we should just relinquish everything and take a nice trip somewhere. And even if he was thinking that, the silent buzz that he noticed within was a clear signal, and of course unequivocally his brain was working, oh yes, he was leaving behind stupid and inconclusive thoughts and meanwhile his brain was working, and focusing, and in the end he would drag the solution from it, the final response, the right answer, that was it: the answer above all: because that sum of sensations and facts had been pressing against his temples as firm and harsh questions, and even the thought of the city rising up within him was a form of question, and in fact if he pricked up his ears, he was distinctly aware of the faint rattle of the rain, even standing at the mirror with his shaving brush, that was it: at that long and disconsolate moment the rain was falling exactly as it had fallen over the previous few days and as it might again on the fifth day, but that was it: what would happen on the fifth day?, at the end of the fourth day whose course he perhaps knew already.

In the post office Paola Lecaldano took a deep breath and inserted the plug into the socket, and of course just a few minutes later out the coffee would come, and she would drink it with Ernesto Cozzolino, of the registered post counter, and with Vincenzo Vecchione, the manager of office number 54, and so to speak she took a look back, and Ernesto Cozzolino was copying the details of a registered letter into the appropriate log with his clear, round hand and Vincenzo Vecchione had already begun the cash-flow statement and was recording all the numbers in a column trying not to go outside the designated boxes, and it was ten o'clock in the morning but in fact the only decent coffee of the day was the one that was about to come out of the espresso machine, and having coffee every morning at about ten o'clock with Cozzolino and Vecchione now seemed a usual and normal everyday matter, yes, you soon get used to things, how soon you get used to them, and now suddenly that realisation of hers was not excessively cheerful, and at that moment she saw herself in the office pouring coffee into cups, of course, what else could she do on such a morning, at around ten o'clock, after starting her work regularly the way she did everything?, what else? She saw herself pouring the coffee into the cups and with a sweet tender secret smile she reflected that Mario, at that moment, was in his second class, maybe geography, he really couldn't stand geography, a stupid notion to make him learn by heart the capitals and the number of inhabitants, and what is the highest summit in the world, what is the deepest point of the sea?, and Kathmandu is inevitably the capital of Nepal. They both woke up at seven o'clock, she ten minutes to in fact, and she went into the kitchen and she put the coffee on the stove with the espresso pot which she had prepared the previous evening, she spent some time looking at her hands in the kitchen by the stove and sometimes when she felt cold she clutched herself with a shiver in her yellow floral dressing gown and put her hands over the gas along with the pot, and she went into his room, and she clearly noticed that smell of him and the bed, she rested the cup on the bedside table, she woke him up a little, look, here's your coffee: oh of course: look, here's your coffee: how many mornings now had she been saying: look, here's your coffee?, it seemed an eternity rather than two years, only two years, twenty-four months, and how many days exactly?, let's think for a minute, three hundred and sixty-five days a year makes seven hundred and seventy in two years, right?, and Mario sat up and reached his hand out towards the cup, and for the first few days she had stood and looked at him, drowsy ruffled likeable as he was, but how many days was it now since she had stopped looking at him with that smiling gaze that she had had when they were engaged?, and in short this life now was a strange one, to think that they had thought of it so often in the past, and they had made plans, and everything looked simple on paper, everything looked easy, and in short let us get it into our heads that for the first three years no children and then we both have to work at having a lovely house, and in fact they worked, yes, they worked, and there was that agony of his that came out when the moment came, and we have to do this, we have to do this, my sweetest love, he said it every time, and for once once only she would have liked to have heard him say from within that he was dying for her and collapse on top of her with his heavy breathing on her shoulder, and that weight, on top of her I wish it would happen, and then in the morning they went into the bathroom one at a time and he immediately shaved and everything, and the house, the house, we have to set up a lovely house, but how strange it is, even with two of us working we can't save a cent, do you imagine we're going to drag our wedding-present furniture with us to the grave?, oh Mario, my sweetest love, somewhere perhaps we made a mistake and we're certainly going on making the same mistake because it isn't possible, it isn't possible, and after shaving he came back out of the bathroom and sat down on the bed and put on his socks, his shirt and everything, and she from the other side of the bed got dressed as well, she put on her stockings and he didn't watch her, why is life like this?, why?, when she had made love with her husband for the first time he had watched her getting dressed in the morning and putting on her stockings, and he had watched her the second time as well, and maybe the third as well, and maybe the fourth as well, but then that was it, then that was it for ever, and why?, why?, what could she do to make the miracle come back?, what could she come up with?, was it possible that anything but feeble lamentation could come out of that rotten useless head of hers?, my God, my God, lovely things have such a short life. And in fact perhaps it isn't work so much, which isn't so demanding in itself, it isn't work so much as the unbearable monotony of days, and days, and there was always getting up like that in the morning and coming home at four, and dinner at eight, and television, and always both of them busy, or tired, and listless, and love had got complicated as well, yes, with that thought that you couldn't do it in the evening, on the grounds that you couldn't make a sound because the people next door hear everything and in short what could you do? Paola Lecaldano glanced outside into the distance, beyond the glass door of the counter, and outside a soft neurasthenic rain was coming down, there were strips of grey in the sky, and nothing to be seen apart from a grey blur, and there was damp in the air, and of course somewhere in some other place there was life, real, dense life that was slipping through her fingers day after day just as it was falling through Mario's fingers, she could see it very clearly: Mario was closing himself away: he was no longer her young lover, her lovely boy, no, now day by day he was becoming a weary man, and Paola Lecaldano heard the coffee gurgling in the machine and she let it go on for a while and then she decided to take it off the heat and with a pot holder that she had brought from home she picked up the pot and poured it into the cups, now they would calmly sip that coffee, and why couldn't she be doing that with Mario right now?, why, the two of them could still have been young and happy if only they had found the time to have coffee together, to look one another in the eye, if that had happened perhaps they would have turned everything upside down, everything completely upside down, work, the house, the plans for new furniture, and what do you expect of the furniture, now there's all this time passing and passing interminably with no meaning and there is this sad awareness from within and that grey sky like yesterday and like tomorrow: it isn't fair, it isn't possible, flowers are budding somewhere on the branches, and there is a strip of light in the morning, somewhere there is our life that we were about to seize, you remember Mario?, which an evil witch hid in a faraway and difficult place, such a difficult place, I really have the sense that we are going round and round in circles, yes, we are turning and turning and always on the same spot and we come back and we leave without ever moving, perhaps it's time to say that's enough, gentlemen, I'm not playing this game any more, but what are you to do, apparently everyone but everyone plays this game, so why be any different?, and who would take the trouble to be different?, and will we really manage to be?, and here we are saying that better times will come, of course, better times are bound to come, you just have to make a few sacrifices and everything will be different, but will it really be different?, I worry that the whole thing is a big swindle, my darling Mario, I'm really afraid that that's how it is, everyone says that better times will come, I agree, but that isn't enough to give me confidence, it isn't nearly enough, because I can see it at home with my own eyes: with every passing day we are extinguished, we are imperceptibly extinguished, and how can we wake up all of a sudden?, how will it be possible to disrupt the order of days and light the flowers of night?, who will give us back the sweet madness of the days of love?, I need to talk to him about it, to tell him all those things out loud, and I will try with all my words to put my case as I must, and of course he will understand, yes, maybe he has understood already maybe these things that I feel and think he thinks too, perhaps he lacks the courage, I can't identify the mistake, but where is the mistake?, where exactly? She stood there looking at the coffee cups, steam rose from the cups to the window pane, outside there was a desolate greyness, in the air in some ways there was a hint of change, it was there in the muscles of your hands, you could spot it in the restless and distracted expression on your face, in your brain that couldn't concentrate, that couldn't linger on a single point, because in fact that persistent question always arose, a confused and inconclusive questioning.

It was just as he finished shaving his neck, on the left-hand side, that Carlo Andreoli had a brainwave: a sudden flash: a thought exploding in your hands: and he smiled at his reflection in the mirror, and briefly he reflected on the past few days and the falling rain that if he pricked his ear he could still hear from down below, he reflected on the collapse on Via Tasso and the chasm in Via Aniello Falcone, and the black-haired dolls, the velvet bands and the floral dress, the sorrowful voice as if of multitudes that had come down from the arrow-holes in the Maschio Angioino to the city. Then all of a sudden everything was clear. Another day would pass, yes, another whole day of rain, and then at dawn on the fifth day tremulous beams of reddish light would appear on the horizon around Capri, and then that light would brighten as the minutes passed, it would turn yellow, and then slowly to white, a different and exactly identical day would be born over the suffering city, the sun would rise and cast its brilliance, the boys would go back into the streets to play football, all the doors of the whole city would be thrown wide open, young women would walk around with shopping bags, the trams would rattle along their tracks to the Riviera di Chiaia, big stray dogs would chase each other in the Villa Comunale, the shops would lift their shutters, all the children in the whole city would run to all the gates of all the schools, in the streets of Port'Alba and Foria there would be the sharp smell of frying, in Mergellina the fishermen would spend long hours repairing their nets, how is it possible, certainly they would raise their heads to look up and they would stand there in the sun, they would stand there because life does not lie in tortuous thoughts, in the falling rain, in the streaks across the sky, life lies in that warm October sun that comes and draws tenderness on every leaf, that distinguishes the green filaments in the garden, that leaves a white line on the line of the sea, and none of any of that, today's question is merely black remorse, a vague question without any meaning, nothing, nothing, it doesn't even exist, and perhaps life would be exactly as it had been before, perhaps no radical disruption would come crashing down to shift the cobbles in the streets and open wounds, the extraordinary event would not take place, it was stupid to imagine that it really might, but you know how it is, sometimes we're suggestible, oh no, not completely, the days would carry on as before along the merciless street, what would be left?, only that faint echo, that melancholy in the half-open eye checking the light. In the indolence of a new day the city would stretch its arms and its back, it would expand its heart to breathe on the gulf, on the hill the sun would draw the outlines of the houses, the perspective of things would not change, no, not for anything in the world. Carlo Andreoli smiled at his own reflection in the mirror. Within him he noticed a new tenderness, an uncontaminated thought. He let the water out of the basin with traces of foam and black dots, and then he ran icy water that he collected in his hands and threw in his face three four five six times, before drying himself he had a moment's hesitation, he paused to notice the water slipping from his eyebrows, from his nose, from his chin, from his ears, he felt it on his skin and inside his brain, that icy regenerating water, and a shiver ran down his spine, with the spongy towel he dried his face and that motionless winking face went on looking, how stupid, my God, how stupid.

Dear readers,

As well as relying on bookshop sales, And Other Stories relies on subscriptions from people like you for many of our books, whose stories other publishers often consider too risky to take on.

Our subscribers don't just make the books physically happen. They also help us approach booksellers, because we can demonstrate that our books already have readers and fans. And they give us the security to publish in line with our values, which are collaborative, imaginative and 'shamelessly literary'.

All of our subscribers:

- receive a first-edition copy of each of the books they subscribe to
- are thanked by name at the end of our subscriber-supported books
- receive little extras from us by way of thank you, for example: postcards created by our authors

BECOME A SUBSCRIBER, OR GIVE A SUBSCRIPTION TO A FRIEND

Visit andotherstories.org/subscribe to help make our books happen. You can subscribe to books we're in the process of making. To purchase books we have already published, we urge you to support your local or favourite bookshop and order directly from them – the often unsung heroes of publishing.

OTHER WAYS TO GET INVOLVED

If you'd like to know about upcoming events and reading groups (our foreign-language reading groups help us choose books to publish, for example) you can:

- join the mailing list at: andotherstories.org/join-us
- follow us on Twitter: @andothertweets
- join us on Facebook: facebook.com/AndOtherStoriesBooks
- follow our blog: andotherstoriespublishing.tumblr.com

This book was made possible thanks to the support of:

Aaron McEnery · Aaron Schneider · Ada Gokay · Adam Barnard · Adam Bowman · Adam Butler · Adam Guy · Adam Lenson · Adriana Diaz Enciso · Aileen-Elizabeth Taylor · Ailsa Peate · Aisling Reina · Ajay Sharma · Alan Donnelly · Alastair Gillespie · Alex Hancock · Alex Ramsey · Alex Robertson · Ali Smith · Alice Fischer · Alice Ramsey · Alice Toulmin · Alison Hughes · Alison Layland · Alison MacConnell · Alison Winston · Allison Graham · Alyse Ceirante · Amanda · Amanda Astley · Amanda Harvey · Amber Da · Amelia Dowe · Ami Zarchi · Amy Rushton · Ana Hincapie · Andrea Reece · Andrew Lees · Andrew Marston · Andrew McCallum · Andrew Rego · Angus Walker · Anna Glendenning · Anna McKee-Poore · Anna Milsom · Anne Carus · Anne Guest · Anneliese O'Malley · Anonymous · Anonymous · Anonymous · Anonymous · Anthony Brown · Anthony Quinn · Anton Muscatelli · Antonia Lloyd-Jones · Antonia Saske · Antonio de Swift · Antony Pearce · Aoife Boyd · Archie Davies · Arwen Smith · Asako Serizawa · Asher Norris · Ashley Hamilton · Audrey Mash · Avril Marren · Barbara Mellor · Barbara & Terry Feller · Barry John Fletcher · Ben Schofield · Ben Thornton · Benjamin Judge · Beth Hancock · Bev Thomas · Beverly Jackson · Bianca Duec · Bianca Jackson · Bianca Winter · Bill Fletcher · Blythe Ridge Sloan · Branka Maricic · Brenda Sully · Briallen Hopper · Brigita Ptackova · Caitlin Halpern · Caitlyn Chappell · Caitriona Lally · Cam Scott · Candida Lacey · Carol Laurent · Carol Mavor · Carolina Pineiro · Caroline Picard · Caroline Rucker · Caroline Waight · Caroline West · Cassidy Hughes · Catherine Barton · Catherine Mansfield · Catherine Taylor · Catriona Gibbs · Cecilia Rossi · Cecilia Uribe · Cecily Maude · Charles Raby · Charlotte Holtam · Charlotte Middleton · Charlotte Murrie & Stephen Charles · Charlotte Whittle · Chenxin Jiang · China Miéville · Chris Ames · Chris Gribble · Chris Hughes · Chris Lintott · Chris McCann · Chris & Kathleen Repper-Day · Chris Stevenson · Christina Moutsou · Christine Brantingham · Christine Ebdy · Christine Luker · Christopher Allen · Ciara Ní Riain · Claire Allison · Claire Brooksby · Claire Malcolm · Claire Tristram · Claire Williams · Clare Archibald · Clare Young · Clarice Borges · Clarice Borges · Clarissa Botsford · Claudia Hoare · Claudia Nannini · Clifford Posner · Clive Bellingham · Clive Hewat · Colin Burrow · Colin Matthews · Courtney Lilly · Craig Barney · Csilla Toldy · Dan Walpole · Dana Behrman · Daniel Arnold · Daniel Coxon · Daniel Douglas · Daniel Gillespie · Daniel Hahn · Daniel Rice · Daniel Stewart · Daniel Sweeney · Daniela Steierberg · Dave Lander · Davi Rocha · David Anderson · David Finlay · David Gavin · David Gould · David Hebblethwaite · David Higgins · David Johnson-Davies · David Jones · David F Long · David Mantero · David Miller · David Shriver · David Smith · David Steege · David Travis · Dawn Leonard · Debbie Pinfold · Deirdre Nic Mhathuna · Denis Stillewagt & Anca Fronescu · Diana Fox Carney · Dinah Bourne · Dominick Santa Cattarina · Dominique Brocard · Duncan Clubb · Duncan Marks · Edward Haxton · Edward Rathke · Elaine Kennedy · Elaine Rassaby · Eleanor Dawson · Eleanor Maier · Elie Howe ·

Elina Zicmane · Elisabeth Cook · Eliza O'Toole · Ellen Coopersmith · Ellen Jones · Ellen Kennedy · Ellen Wilkinson · Elly Zelda Goldsmith · Emily Chia & Marc Ronnie · Emily Taylor · Emily Yaewon Lee & Gregory Limpens · Emma Barraclough · Emma Bielecki · Emma Perry · Emma Pope · Emma Yearwood · Emma Louise Grove · Eric E Rubeo · Erin Grace Cobby · Eva Kostyu · Ewan Tant · Finbarr Farragher · Finlay McEwan · Finnuala Butler · Florian Duijsens · Fran Sanderson · Frances Hazelton · Francesca Brooks · Francesca Fanucci · Francis Taylor · Freya Warren · Friederike Knabe · Gabriela Lucia Garza de Linde · Gabrielle Crockatt · Gary Gorton · Gavin Smith · Gawain Espley · Gemma Tipton · Geoff Copps · Geoff Thrower · Geoffrey Cohen · Geoffrey Urland · George Christie · George Wilkinson · Gerard Mehigan · Gill Boag-Munroe · Gillian Ackroyd · Gillian Bohnet · Gillian Grant · Gillian Spencer · Gordon Cameron · Graham R Foster · Guy Haslam · Hadil Balzan · Hank Pryor · Hannah Mayblin · Hannah Richter · Hannah Stevens · Hans Lazda · Harriet Spicer · Helen Barker · Helen Brady · Helen Snow · Helen Swain · Helen White · Helen Wormald · Henrike Laehnemann · Henry Asson · Howard Robinson · Hugh Gilmore · Iain Munro · Ian Barnett · Ian McMillan · Ian Smith · Íde Corley · Ingrid Olsen · Irene Mansfield · Isabel Adey · Isabella Garment · Isabella Weibrecht · Istvan Szatmari · J Collins · Jacinta Perez Gavilan Torres · Jack Brown · Jacqueline Lademann · Jacqueline Ting Lin · James Beck · James Cubbon · James Lesniak · James Mewis · James Portlock · James Scudamore · James Tierney · James Wilper · Jamie Mollart · Jamie Walsh · Jane Leuchter · Jane Livingstone · Jane Woollard · Janette Ryan · Janika Urig · Jasmine Gideon · JC Sutcliffe · Jean Pierre de Rosnay · Jean-Jacques Regouffre · Jeehan Quijano · Jeff Collins · Jennifer Bernstein · Jennifer Higgins · Jennifer O'Brien · Jenny Booth · Jenny Huth · Jenny Newton · Jenny Nicholls · Jenny Yang · Jeremy Morton · Jeremy Weinstock · Jerry Simcock · Jess Howard-Armitage · Jessica Billington · Jethro Soutar · Jillian Jones · Jo Bell · Jo Harding · Jo Lateu · Joan O'Malley · Joanna Flower · Joanna Luloff · Joao Pedro Bragatti Winckler · Jodie Adams · Joel Love · Joelle Skilbeck · Johan Forsell · Johan Trouw · John Berube · John Conway · John Down · John Gent · John Hodgson · John Kelly · John McGill · John McKee · John Royley · John Shaw · John Steigerwald · John Winkelman · Jon Riches · Jon Talbot · Jonathan Blaney · Jonathan Kiehlmann · Jonathan Ruppin · Jonathan Watkiss · Joseph Camilleri · Joseph Cooney · Joseph Huennekens · Joseph Schreiber · Joshua Davis · Joshua McNamara · Judyth Emanuel · Julia Hays · Julia Hobsbawm · Julia Hoskins · Julian Duplain · Julian Lomas · Julie Gibson · Julie Gibson · Julie-Ann Griffiths · Juliet Swann · JW Mersky · Kaarina Hollo · Karen Waloschek · Karl Kleinknecht & Monika Motylinska · Kasper Haakansson · Kasper Hartmann · Kate Attwooll · Kate Griffin · Katharina Herzberger · Katharine Freeman · Katharine Robbins · Katherine El-Salahi · Katherine Mackinnon · Katherine Parish · Kathleen Magone · Kathryn Edwards · Kathryn Lewis · Katie Brown · Katrina Thomas · Katriona Macpherson · Keith Walker · Kevin Porter · Khairunnisa Ibrahim · Kirsteen Smith · Kirsten Major · KL Ee · Klara Rešetič · Krystine Phelps · Kuaam Animashaun · Lana Selby · Lander Hawes ·

Laura Batatota · Laura Clarke · Laura Lea · Laura Waddell · Lauren Ellemore · Laurence Laluyaux · Leonie Schwab · Leonie Smith · Leri Price · Lesley Lawn · Lesley Watters · Leslie Wines · Liliana Lobato · Linda Walz · Lindsay Brammer · Lindsey Ford · Liz Ketch · Liz Sage · Lizzie Broadbent · Lizzie Coulter · Lochlan Bloom · Lola Boorman · Loretta Platts · Lorna Bleach · Lorna Scott Fox · Lottie Smith · Louisa Hare · Louise Curtin · Louise Musson · Louise Piper · Luc Verstraete · Lucia Rotheray · Lucy Moffatt · Lucy Phillips · Lucy Summers · Lynda Graham · Lynn Martin · M Manfre · Madeline Teevan · Maeve Lambe · Mahan L Ellison & K Ashley Dickson · Mal Campbell · Mandy Wight · Manja Pflanz · Marcella Morgan · Marcus Joy · Marie Cloutier · Marie Donnelly · Marina Castledine · Marina Galanti · Marja S Laaksonen · Mark Lumley · Mark Sargent · Mark Sztyber · Mark Waters · Marlene Adkins · Martha Gifford · Martha Nicholson · Martha Stevns · Martin Boddy · Martin Brampton · Martin Nathan · Martin Vosyka · Martin Whelton · Mary Carozza · Mary Wang · Marzieh Youssefi · Matt & Owen Davies · Matt Klein · Matthew Armstrong · Matthew Black · Matthew Francis · Matthew Geden · Matthew Smith · Matthew Thomas · Matthew Warshauer · Matthew Woodman · Matty Ross · Maureen Pritchard · Max Cairnduff · Max Longman · Meaghan Delahunt · Megan Taylor · Megan Wittling · Meike Schwamborn · Melissa Beck · Melissa Quignon-Finch · Meredith Jones · Meredith Martin · Michael Andal · Michael James Eastwood · Michael Gavin · Michael Johnston · Michele Keyaert · Michelle Lotherington · Michelle Roberts · Miranda Gold · Miranda Persaud · Molly Foster · Monika Olsen · Morag Campbell · Morven Dooner · Myles Nolan · N Tsolak · Namita Chakrabarty · Nancy Oakes · Natalie Smith · Nathalie Atkinson · Neil Pretty · Nicholas Brown · Nick Chapman · Nick James · Nick Nelson & Rachel Eley · Nick Sidwell · Nick Williams · Nicola Hart · Nicola Mira · Nicola Sandiford · Nicole Matteini · Nigel Palmer · Nikki Sinclair · Nikolaj Ramsdal Nielsen · Nina Alexandersen · Nina Moore · Nina Power · Noah Levin · Octavia Kingsley · Olga Alexandru · Olga Zilberbourg · Olivia Payne · Pam Madigan · Pashmina Murthy · Pat Crowe · Patricia Appleyard · Patricia Hughes · Patrick McGuinness · Patrick Owen · Paul Bailey · Paul Cray · Paul Daw · Paul Howe & Ally Hewitt · Paul Jones · Paul Munday · Paul Robinson · Paula Edwards · Penelope Hewett Brown · Perlita Payne · Peter McCambridge · Peter Rowland · Peter Vos · Philip Carter · Philip Warren · Phyllis Reeve · Piet Van Bockstal · PRAH Foundation · Rachael Williams · Rachel Bambury · Rachel Beddow · Rachel Carter · Rachel Hinkel · Rachel Lasserson · Rachel Matheson · Rachel Van Riel · Rachel Watkins · Rachele Huennekens · Rebecca Braun · Rebecca Carter · Rebecca Moss · Rebecca Roadman · Rebecca Rosenthal · Rebekah Hughes · Réjane Collard-Walker · Rhiannon Armstrong · Rhodri Jones · Richard Ashcroft · Richard Bauer · Richard Gwyn · Richard Harrison · Richard Mansell · Richard Priest · Richard Shea · Richard Shore · Richard Soundy · Richard John Davis · Rita Hynes · RM Foord · Robert Downing · Robert Gillett · Robert Norman · Robin Patterson · Robin Taylor · Ronan Cormacain · Rory Williamson · Rosanna Foster · Rose Arnold · Rowena McWilliams · Roz Simpson · Rupert Ziziros · S Altinel · S Italiano · S Wight · Sabrina Uswak · Sally

Baker · Sally Dowell · Sam Gordon · Sam Norman · Sam Ruddock · Samantha Smith · Sarah Arboleda · Sarah Benson · Sarah Butler · Sarah Lippek · Sarah Lucas · Sarah Pybus · Sarah Wollner · Scott Thorough · Sean Kelly · Sean Malone · Sean McGivern · Sez Kiss · Shannon Beckner · Shannon Knapp · Shawn Moedl · Sheridan Marshall · Shira Lob · Shirley Harwood · Sian Rowe · Sigurjon Sigurdsson · Silvia Kwon · Simon Robertson · Simone O'Donovan · SK Grout · Sofia Hardinger · Sonia Crites · Sonia Overall · Sophia Wickham · Sophie Bowley-Aicken · Sophie Goldsworthy · Sophy Roberts · ST Dabbagh · Stacy Rodgers · Stefanie May IV · Stephan Eggum · Stephanie Lacava · Stephen Coade · Stephen Pearsall · Steven & Gitte Evans · Stuart Wilkinson · Sue Little · Sue & Ed Aldred · Susan Ferguson · Susan Higson · Susie Roberson · Suzanne Fortey · Suzanne Lee · Swannee Welsh · Sylvie Zannier-Betts · Tamar Shlaim · Tamara Larsen · Tammi Owens · Tammy Watchorn · Tania Hershman · Ted Burness · Teresa Griffiths · Terry Kurgan · The Mighty Douche Softball Team · The Rookery In the Bookery · Thees Spreckelsen · Thomas Bell · Thomas Chadwick · Thomas Fritz · Thomas Mitchell · Thomas van den Bout · Tiffany Lehr · Tim Theroux · Timothy Harris · Tina Rotherham-Winqvist · TJ Clark · Toby Ryan · Tom Darby · Tom Franklin · Tom Gray · Tom Wilbey · Tony Bastow · Tony Messenger · Torna Russell-Hills · Tory Jeffay · Tracy Bauld · Tracy Lee-Newman · Tracy Shapley · Trevor Lewis · Trevor Wald · Tricia Durdey · Val Challen · Vanessa Dodd · Vanessa Jones · Vanessa Nolan · Vanessa Rush · Victor Meadowcroft · Victoria Adams · Victoria Seaman · Vijay Pattisapu · Virginia Weir · Visaly Muthusamy · Wendy Langridge · Wendy Peate · Wenna Price · Will Huxter · William Dennehy · William Schwaber · Zoe Stephenson · Zoe Taylor · Zoe Thomas · Zoë Brasier

Current & Upcoming Books

01 Juan Pablo Villalobos, *Down the Rabbit Hole*
translated from the Spanish by Rosalind Harvey

02 Clemens Meyer, *All the Lights*
translated from the German by Katy Derbyshire

03 Deborah Levy, *Swimming Home*

04 Iosi Havilio, *Open Door*
translated from the Spanish by Beth Fowler

05 Oleg Zaionchkovsky, *Happiness is Possible*
translated from the Russian by Andrew Bromfield

06 Carlos Gamerro, *The Islands*
translated from the Spanish by Ian Barnett

07 Christoph Simon, *Zbinden's Progress*
translated from the German by Donal McLaughlin

08 Helen DeWitt, *Lightning Rods*

09 Deborah Levy, *Black Vodka: ten stories*

10 Oleg Pavlov, *Captain of the Steppe*
translated from the Russian by Ian Appleby

11 Rodrigo de Souza Leão, *All Dogs are Blue*
translated from the Portuguese by Zoë Perry & Stefan Tobler

12 Juan Pablo Villalobos, *Quesadillas*
translated from the Spanish by Rosalind Harvey

13 Iosi Havilio, *Paradises*
translated from the Spanish by Beth Fowler

14 Ivan Vladislavić, *Double Negative*

15 Benjamin Lytal, *A Map of Tulsa*

16 Ivan Vladislavić, *The Restless Supermarket*

17 Elvira Dones, *Sworn Virgin*
translated from the Italian by Clarissa Botsford

37 Various, *Lunatics, Lovers and Poets: Twelve Stories after Cervantes and Shakespeare*

38 Yuri Herrera, *The Transmigration of Bodies*
translated from the Spanish by Lisa Dillman

39 César Aira, *The Seamstress and the Wind*
translated from the Spanish by Rosalie Knecht

40 Juan Pablo Villalobos, *I'll Sell You a Dog*
translated from the Spanish by Rosalind Harvey

41 Enrique Vila-Matas, *Vampire in Love*
translated from the Spanish by Margaret Jull Costa

42 Emmanuelle Pagano, *Trysting*
translated from the French by Jennifer Higgins and Sophie Lewis

43 Arno Geiger, *The Old King in His Exile*
translated from the German by Stefan Tobler

44 Michelle Tea, *Black Wave*

45 César Aira, *The Little Buddhist Monk*
translated from the Spanish by Nick Caistor

46 César Aira, *The Proof*
translated from the Spanish by Nick Caistor

47 Patty Yumi Cottrell, *Sorry to Disrupt the Peace*

48 Yuri Herrera, *Kingdom Cons*
translated from the Spanish by Lisa Dillman

49 Fleur Jaeggy, *I am the Brother of XX*
translated from the Italian by Gini Alhadeff

50 Iosi Havilio, *Petite Fleur*
translated from the Spanish by Lorna Scott Fox

51 Juan Tomás Ávila Laurel, *The Gurugu Pledge*
translated from the Spanish by Jethro Soutar

52 Joanna Walsh, *Worlds from the Word's End*

53 César Aira, *The Lime Tree*
translated from the Spanish by Chris Andrews

54 Nicola Pugliese, *Malacqua*
translated from Italian by Shaun Whiteside

55 Ann Quin, *The Unmapped Country*

NICOLA PUGLIESE was born in Milan in 1944, but lived almost all his life in Naples. A journalist, his first and only novel, *Malacqua*, was published in 1977 by Italo Calvino. It sold out in days, but, at the author's request, was never reprinted until after his death in 2012.

SHAUN WHITESIDE's translations from Italian include *Q*, *54*, *Manituana* and *Altai* by Luther Blissett/Wu Ming Foundation, *The Solitude of Prime Numbers* by Paolo Giordano and *Venice is a Fish* and *Stabat Mater* by Tiziano Scarpa. He also translates from French, German and Dutch. He lives in London.